This book is to b...
the last da...

13. OCT. 1992

Macmillan *Pacesetters*

1   Arrival

It was without regret that I took the Picadilly line from Finsbury Park to Heathrow Airport that cold English evening. England is one of those countries where you can live for many years and still not get used to the cold weather. One might have thought that for an African like myself, who had lived two decades in London, the biting wind of autumn would have been no problem, but I have never got used to it. Well, come to think of it, even the native black and white English whose parents and grandparents were born in Britain never got used to it. All of us still wrap ourselves in woollens and mufflers and mutter, 'Cold isn't it?' It only goes to show that nobody really gets used to anything bad — and the British early winter or late autumn winds could be that bad.

I tumbled into the main building at Heathrow, puffing from the cold and from lugging my luggage with me. The clerk at the counter wanted to know what my hand-luggage was going to weigh, and I had to tell her, as patiently as I could, that she should not worry about it. There are so many things about us those foreign girls do not know. The fact that our hand-luggage can sometimes weigh more than our actual luggage is beyond their wildest imagination. To us hand-luggage means hand-luggage even though we have to drag it most of the time. For if we do not do that what will we tell all those relatives and friends who come to greet us on arrival? A woman in her prime cannot go around saying to friends that she could not bring a doll for Sikira or a jogging suit for Latifu, or a new velvet skull-cap for the Alhaji, simply because a skinny airways clerk insisted that she should only carry five kilos in her hand-luggage. Those people who made the law did not take into account the gregariousness of the Woman from Africa.

Home at last after I argued my way through Customs and were all my troubles not worth my while, for who should be there at the huge Murtala Muhammed Airport in Lagos, smiling with puffy cheeks and eyes that sparkled, but my sister-in-law Amina and her husband Nurudeen. Amina was so happy that her full cheeks seemed about to cover her eyes up. Her elaborate hair-do was a little on the conspicuous side as usual, but who cared. She rushed towards me with arms wide in welcome and we embraced. She was over the moon with joy and I was really glad to see her looking so well and glamorous. My dour-looking brother stood with his arms folded, stolidly watching us embrace each other. He looked nonchalant, as if he was not part of the scene, as if he was not happy at my coming to visit them, as if my being there was no business of his whatsoever.

'Aren't you happy to see me, Nurudeen?' I cried over Amina's shoulder.

'Of course, I am. What in the name of Allah do you want me to do? Walk over on my hands, just because you're here? Do you know how long we have been waiting for that plane of yours?' He laughed a low mirthless laugh, throwing his well-shaped head back as he did so.

I looked at him, amused at his manly role-playing. All this display, simply to show how emotionally tough he was. Well my brother was tough-looking that evening with his sparkling *agbada* lace and matching skull-cap, with his shiny flat shoes, gold chain and gold watch. Oh, Nigerian men do love to look good, and when it came to welcoming their relatives at Murtala Muhammed Airport, some of them really went to town. I looked almost undressed in my grey Marks and Spencer's tweed skirt and silk blouse. Who could blame me — it had been freezing when I left London, though now in Lagos it felt as if I was putting my head into a mildly heated oven. Such a contrast, London and Lagos, and yet most of us travel to and fro between these two big cities.

'All these bits and pieces,' my brother grumbled as he helped the porter load my bags into the boot of his Nigeria-assembled Peugeot.

As we backed our way out of the tangled mess of cars and drove out on to the highway, my sister-in-law started to look this way and that as if she was about to impart something secretive. Then she nudged my side and said, 'Auntie Bintu, you know some people have a way of stimulating stories, just as some babies bring luck with them at birth? I think you are one of those people who encourage others to tell you stories. Don't you think so, Auntie Bintu?'

I nodded as we both involuntarily glanced in my brother's direction. His straight back seemed so uncompromising and he was now wearing that air of suffering he enjoyed putting on when we, his female relatives, were around. Amina looked back at me and as her face creased in suppressed amusement her expression told me in that silent, dimpled smile,

'Don't worry, I know you're a good listener, and I shall tell it all to you by and by.'

I got the message but it had reawakened my curiosity, so much so that the cool evening landscape from Murtala Muhammed to the satellite city in Lagos seemed simply to be going through me. I became impatient. Amina was good at recounting events. She was good at bringing me up to date on any happenings, however trivial, that I had missed since my last visit. I wanted to hear what she had to say. The last story she had told me about Ramonu was still ringing in my ears. I would never forget till my dying day the gripping feeling that sad story had given me. Now she was bursting with a new one. I could hardly wait.

But wait I must, as relatives and friends poured into my brother's modern living room to welcome me. They came to enquire about my family in England and wanted to know everything about my welfare. Some came to ask about their relatives — relatives who had not written to them for months. I had to reassure everybody that we were all well, that the cold in England had not killed us yet, that no, Enoch Powell no longer made his 'River of Babylon' speeches, that his place had now been taken by some half-wits who called themselves the 'National Front'.

'National Front, national front! So we should start our own national front here too. Do you know how many thousands of white British live here in Nigeria? Look at all our universities, our book trade and our building trade, they are in all of them. We let them stay there, give them the best houses!' my brother cried from behind the fridge where he was mixing us some cold drinks.

'Oh, I shouldn't start that here. Two wrongs can never make a right,' I began hesitantly.

'Sometimes, it is good to teach these white people sense. Just send them all packing, just as we did to those Ghanaians who were getting too big for their boots,' Amina said supporting her husband.

'I did not like that at all. It was a disgrace. It was a big minus in Nigeria's list of good behaviour. We should not do things like that to one another,' I said, my voice unconsciously raised.

My brother brought out the drinks and distributed the glasses. 'I wonder sometimes about what has happened to Ghana. Do you know that a few years ago a Ghanaian would fight you if you made the mistake of calling him a Nigerian? Now just look how the tables have turned — all in my life time,' my brother remarked, looking thoughtful.

We all kept quiet for a while after this obvious statement. We all knew that what was happening in Ghana could occur anywhere in black Africa if one's government was not careful.

Then my cousin, silver-haired Alhaji Gurudi, said aloud what I thought wrapped the whole conversation in a neat packet. 'The more reason we should treat them with consideration. Because today it is Ghana, so why should it not be Nigeria tomorrow? Allah knows best.'

All this was getting too heavy and morbid for that perfect hostess, Amina. She smiled and dimpled at everybody and hurried up to the Alhaji with a well-wrapped present. 'Your cousin, my Auntie Bintu, brought this for you from the country of the white people.'

The Alhaji, who previously had been showing signs

of wanting to leave the room, stopped in his stride, raised his hands as if giving a benediction and prayed for me. 'You will always return in safety. You will always return because Allah will always guide you and his chosen servant Mohammed will always plead for you. I thank you very much.' He bowed gracefully, gathered his *agbada* around him and left the room. I was now happy that I had paid that visit to the sales in one of our local shops where I was lucky enough to get several of the Tommy Cooper red felt caps favoured by many of our Alhajis.

One by one my friends and relatives left, this one with a packet of handkerchiefs, that one with a head-scarf, another with a doll for her little girl. My sister-in-law beamed with satisfaction. She loved giving things to people as it enhanced her position in her local community in Festac city of Lagos.

'You must be tired,' my brother Nurudeen said, after giving way to a rather exaggerated yawn with which he told us that it was time for us to go to bed. I was tired, yes, but somehow I resented being ordered to bed as if I were a child. His wife Amina could take it, but for some reason now that all the friends and relatives had left, I wasn't too tired to be sociable. So I pretended that I had not seen the gaping yawn.

Then he turned to his wife and said sharply, 'Are you going to watch that stupid dancer all night? You have to get the children ready for school tomorrow, remember?'

'Oh no, I am not going to watch her all night. You are tired as you have been driving all the way to Ekpe whilst we stay at home.'

He got up, put on his dour, long-suffering look and made for his bedroom, which he called the master

6

bedroom. We could hear him grumbling, 'As if I can afford to forget!'

Amina busied herself getting us a glass of cold chocolate drink and hissed as she sat down by me, 'Madam Ubakanma's daughter-in-law has given birth to two boys. The two women are doing the almost impossible, they are keeping a new kind of family going, they are starting another generation of Ubakanmas. I raise my drink to them.' Amina raised her mug of chocolate drink. Instinctively, I did the same even though I hadn't the faintest clue as to what she was talking about.

'Look Amina,' I managed to interrupt as we gulped our chilled cocoa, 'you have a way of talking in riddles. You introduce something so abruptly and you expect everybody to follow - and not only to follow but to read your thoughts as well! I am neither a magician nor a mind-reader, you know.'

'Oh, Auntie,' she said in her rather forced stage whisper, her round brown eyes dancing from side to side. 'I told you at the airport that you brought a story with you. Your brother, my husband, and I went to see the twins. They cried with so much force and energy that one could hear their strong voices even before one entered their beautiful Surulere flat. They looked so healthy — just as if they had been born singly and had not had to share the same womb for nine months. And Madam Maria Ubakanma has never looked so young since I first knew her. They were so happy. Her daughter-in-law, such a nice girl, simply glowed. I hope they remain like that for ever.' She sighed deeply as if talking to herself. And for a little while her brown lustrous eyes were clouded and sad. Then as quickly as she had plunged into this

7

temporary gloom, she snapped out of it and announced in a lighter, brighter tone, 'Well she is young, she is educated, and soon she may marry again and leave Maria Ubakanma to take care of the twins. That would be sad, but it may not be too sad, because the two women are doing the impossible. They are going to achieve what George Ubakanma failed to achieve through his sons, Charles and the unlucky Afam. And they will succeed. You mark my words Auntie Bintu, they will succeed. I am so glad our women are now doing something, especially the educated ones. They have been too silent and too obedient for far too long. I am glad they are changing. They said we used to be like that in old Africa. Those women then could keep families going when their menfolk had gone. But now people would say that a family like that is not a family, and that that kind of arrangement is not a marriage. What Auntie Bintu, is a marriage, and what is a family?'

'Amina, Amina,' I called gently. This startled her. It had looked for a while as if she had thought that she was talking to herself, all alone. She collected herself and laughed suddenly with pure relief. Her laughter cut through the night like a knife. It was not loud, but it was rather penetrating — so much so that my brother's voice cut through our inattention.

'You mean we are not going to get any sleep in this house tonight?' he asked in an injured tone.

I got up, yawned a big yawn almost as big as Nurudeen's and said, 'Amina I guess he is right. It has been a long day. And I have not the faintest idea what you are talking about. You are going to tell me something about the Ubakanma family. But I don't think I know who they are or what they have done or why they had twins. It is too late to start right now, however. Tomorrow will do, my dear wife.'

'You mean we should go to the Murtala Muhammed Highway again and stay there in my car,just as we did when I told you the story of Ramonu and his naira?' Amina asked, smiling mischievously.

'No,' I replied, laughing quietly as my mind conjured up again the terrible picture of Ramonu's demise. 'That would be rather dramatic. We can stay here when the children have gone to school. Then you must tell me all.'

'Well,' Amina said with obvious misgiving, 'I hope we have fewer well-wishers tomorrow, otherwise I will have to spend my time in the kitchen frying meat for relatives who have come to see you.'

'If it becomes impossible, we'll go out and eat somewhere.'

'Eh, Auntie Bintu! Your brother won't like that! Us going to eat like women with no husbands!'

'If my brother should find out, I will simply have to tell him that we needed some peace and quiet to talk. And moreover, Amina, I am running out of presents. I could only carry so much!'

'Auntie-e-e-e, Auntie Bintu, you're something else. Yes, tomorrow we'll pretend we're going marketing and then we'll go and eat somewhere. I am so excited.'

I knew that I was not going to pretend. She must have worked all day getting the house ready for my visit and for the relatives she knew would come to see me. I did not see anything wrong in eating out as long as we returned before the children came back from school. I did not see any unfaithfulness in that. I was becoming rather impatient with our women for letting men get their way all the time. Men go for

9

drinks, they eat out and some take other women out. So why should it be wrong for two sisters to eat out if they could afford it? People would accuse me of teaching a younger woman bad ways, but I did not think it was bad at all and Amina was not a fool; she knew it was going to be a harmless relaxation. Amina could tell her husband what she liked, but, if asked, I was going to tell my brother Nurudeen where we had gone. As far as I am concerned, eating out does not make women prostitutes or render us unfaithful. Women are people just like men, and without men customers, I'm quite sure there'd be no female prostitutes.

With that determination ringing in my ears and singing in my mind, I slipped into a deep refreshing sleep, ignoring the humming air-conditioner, and those peculiar little noises that make Lagos what it is — a town that seldom sleeps.

2 Business Women

The humming noise from the air-conditioner soon
penetrated into my sub-consciousness, and I became
fully awake. As the early morning sound filtered into
the darkened room in which I had spent the night,
I decided that the best thing would be for me to lie
quite still until Amina had finished getting her
children off to school and my brother off to work.

I must have slipped back into sleep, for I felt
somebody shaking me and when I opened my eyes I
saw her standing there, smiling. 'Good morning
Auntie Bintu, you must have been very tired. Do you
know that you slept through the children's noises?
They have all gone now and the rest of the day is
ours.'

As she said this, the wall clock in their living room
chimed nine o'clock. 'Is it really nine o'clock?' I cried.
'Now is that nine o'clock or ten o'clock London time?
Fancy my sleeping all this long. You are right,
Amina, I must have been very tired. I'm normally
writing or lecturing by this time in London.'

Before Amina left my room, she turned and said,
'I hope, Auntie, that you have not forgotten that we
are eating out today.' Her voice was wistfully
expectant like that of a child looking forward to an
outing. I did not ask her whether she thought my
brother would be angry with her. She'd probably

reconciled herself to it, and who knows what she might have told her husband in the course of the night so that he would have realised that there was nothing wrong in our going out to eat.

'I know the very place you'll like. It's off Murtala Muhammed Highway. It's not very big but we'll have a choice of Hausa, Efik, Yoruba or Ibo food and they are all well cooked,' Amina added.

I got ready by putting on the one and only Nigerian outfit which I had brought from London with me. I suspected that it looked a little dated, since I had bought it in Calabar two years previously. I intended to update my wardrobe by and by because, despite the fact that Nigeria has fewer seasonal changes in the year, I have not come across many other places where fashion changes so rapidly, and someone who continually wears outdated though perfect clothes is dubbed old-fashioned. A tag like that would not do my relative's ego any good at all.

'Oh Auntie Bintu, is that what you're wearing?' Amina exclaimed on seeing me. Her face wore a peculiar mixture of mischief and amusement.

'Isn't it good? Don't you like it? We have to shop tomorrow so that I can buy the latest fashions. In England, I don't follow fashion. I just wear whatever makes me comfortable and warm. Here one must be careful, I know.'

Amina nodded, agreeing with me. 'Here one must be careful. You see over there they say you cover your best clothes with top coats, so that it does not matter whether you wear anything underneath . . .'

'Ah, Amina that is not quite true, I must say. We do wear things underneath and you do take your top coats off when you reach your destination . . . People

12

do exaggerate sometimes. Is this outfit too shameful then?'

Amina started to laugh. Her puffy cheeks became full and they seemed to explode into uncontrollable mirth. It was a laughter that was so infectious that I had to join in, laughing at what I did not know.

I was wearing the blouse and long skirt made from *abada* cloth. I had worn it many times but could not bring myself to throw it away, simply because I had bought it two years back. It was supposed to be a modern African fashion, which cuts across tribe and class, though, a long time ago, it used to be worn mainly by people from the Ibo and Urobobo tribes. Westernising the same material by making it into a blouse and long skirt outfit gave it its Calabar touch.

'I know,' Amina announced presently. She had probably had a sudden brain-wave. 'I know,' she repeated, pressing her forefinger against her round, shiny lips. 'I have a suit almost like that. You remember you bought me one from Calabar. I am going to put mine on, then we will both look like two women from the East married to a rich husband and eating out in style.'

Before I had time to think of what to say or do, my sister-in-law hurried into the bedroom she shared with her husband and her three-year-old son, Muftao. I opened my mouth to make a protest that she did not have to dress in a down-and-out fashion, simply not to show me up. But Amina did not wait to listen. I know that it is the thing to suffer relatives. You can shake off bad friends or unsavoury acquaintances, but embarrassing relatives are part of your make-up. By dressing down Amina was determined not to show me up as an outdated, fashionless so-and-so. It was her way of bearing part of a relative's burden.

I should not have worried because Amina came out soon after looking really gorgeous in her own suit. Hers was made of *abada* that had a red background with leaves done in white in the foreground. She had added white accessories to emphasise the whites in the material. With her expensive hairdo, the whole outfit all became her very well. Despite all her efforts to look old-fashioned, I still looked like her housekeeper or her children's nurse.

My suit had a brown background. I had chosen this colour purposely so that I could wear it in England. Though it had tiny yellow stars on it to relieve the brownness, against the bright tropical Lagos background it looked a little on the dark side. And as if that was not enough to show my out-of-touchness, my hair, which was done for me by my Caribbean hairdresser in London, was too Westernised to go with our general turnout. For a while I felt not only out of touch and out of date but out of place as well.

Amina was smiling triumphantly and at the same time watching and registering all the workings on my face. She was trying to change her intense expression when I caught her at it; it was too late for I could read my sister-in-law like a book. Beginning to feel fed-up I volunteered, 'Suppose we wait until I have done my shopping, eh Amina?'

Amina's eyes danced in exaggerated fear. 'No Auntie Bintu, please don't do that. People will start coming and I will have to be in the kitchen all day. Let's go now. You do look nice, you really do; well a bit foreign, but that is the truth, isn't it? After all you have only just returned. It is still fashionable to be a been-to, though every Tom, Dick and Harry now goes to London. London still has its glamour, especially when people know that you have stayed there so long,' Amina finished consolingly.

'How will they know all that just by looking at me?' I asked.

'Oh Auntie Bintu let's go. Anybody can tell. It is not a bad thing,' she drawled in a voice that was too indulgent to hurt too much.

To avoid saying 'good morning' and answering innumerable questions from her kind neighbours, Amina insisted that we leave through the back door.

'But why? I like saying good morning and talking to people, Amina!' I cried in protest.

'I like it too, Auntie. The problem is that we may let it slip out of our mouths that we are eating at the Ikorodu Hotel, then tongues will start to wag. It is better for them not to know, then we don't need to lie about our destination'.

So Amina had not told her husband about our little escapade. I did not mind either way. If anybody asked me I was going to say exactly what happened.

Her red Volkswagen looked tattier than I had remembered. One could understand the rapid deterioration of cars in Lagos after a run along one of the roads. For quite a large part of the year some of these roads were under water. And as for the general mode of driving, it still left a great deal to be desired, though I felt it was improving, maybe due to the stringent laws and the oil glut. I could not tell for certain. Maybe I was gradually getting used to Nigerian roads. But whatever it was that was responsible for the slight improvement in road manners, I think that the criticisms of Nigeria by

Nigerians themselves, and the world media at large, had gone towards this improvement. One of the joys of being a Nigerian is this freedom of speech which everybody is allowed. A beggar in the street can say whatever he likes about his country's president, and still go on begging. This attitude is one which people in many parts of Africa find baffling to the point of admiring us Nigerians. Few countries in Black Africa enjoy such democracy.

Though it was not raining, yet it was still very wet and muddy on the roads. Amina's Volkswagen Beetle squelched through the littered grimy side roads and along the cluttered streets where the sole repositories for household rubbish appeared to be the open gutters. Nonetheless we squelched on and after a rather sharp turn, came face to face with a beautiful house, one that the owner seemed to have managed to deposit there right in the middle of this slum-like environment. The huge house sat squarely, looking not dissimilar to the ones you see on holiday brochures. It was a two-storey affair painted a cream colour; all the woodwork was green. There were dwarf palms in front, and the gates were wide enough to take in two cars at the same time. Inside the front courtyard there was a shed, and in that shed there were several men already drinking at that time in the morning.

We drove into the courtyard, and we could feel the eyes of the men boring into us. 'They probably think we are "business women",' laughed Amina as she parked her car near to a smaller house which had the word 'Office' inscribed on a placard in front of its door.

'So what's bad about being business women?' I asked.

'Not business, I mean the other one,' Amina

explained, giggling like a schoolgirl bent on breaking the school rules.

'I don't know what you mean. We are here to eat and to hell with what the men think.'

'Oh, Auntie Bintu, it's so nice to go out with you. You sometimes talk like men. That is why I want to tell you the story of the Ubakanmas.'

As we stepped out of the parking lot, a young boy in a cream shirt and khaki trousers ran up to us and demanded, 'Yes, Madam?'

I saw that Amina was at a temporary loss as to what to say when faced with this unusual efficiency. So I said quickly, 'Please show us the restaurant.'

'You wait here for the Oga, or you wait outside, here?' he asked, pointing to the shed.

'We are not waiting for any Master or Oga. We came on our own,' I cried.

'Sorry madam, I know watting you wan' make you come.'

We followed the bandy-legged waiter or man-of-all-works or whatever he was. I thought I saw a place with 'restaurant' written on its door as he led us on, but I thought I should keep quiet and follow this charade to its finale. Then he opened the door to a large room with a huge well-made bed in it, and motioned us to sit on the two chairs arranged militarily along the wall. I looked at Amina and she looked at me, and before we could say a word, the boy pressed a button and some ear-deafening music started to blare out. He motioned us again to sit down and mouthed the words 'Master Oga' once more. He was on the verge of leaving us when I clutched at his sleeve and mouthed, 'Are you deaf? We want to eat, not to, emm, wait for any silly Oga.'

Amina seemed to have been seized with a fit of uncontrollable laughter. She collected herself a little and started to put her fingers into her mouth to show the young man that we were there to eat. He looked at us with a puzzled expression. He looked anew at our long *abada* skirts and scarfless heads as Amina's gesticulations became really frantic. She started to say, 'Chop, chop, chop,' at the top of her voice, at the same time as motioning towards her mouth.

'Ah!' The young man cocked his head to one side. 'Na only chop, chop you want, no business at all, at all?'

'Right,' we sang with relief. 'Na chop, chop we want, no business.'

He led us out again into the open and I asked, 'But look young man, why the loud music?'

'Ah,' he explained wearing a knowing expression, 'that one na part of the thirty naira, wey we de charge for one hour. Many customers de like am with fine, fine music.'

Thirty naira, that was about twenty-eight pounds sterling, I calculated mentally. To spend all that simply to rent a room for an hour. 'Okay, o, we no business customers, we be chop, chop one,' I said aloud, lapsing into the pidgin English of my youth.

We eventually sat at a table and, when he left, Amina started to laugh again; this time I joined in the amusement.

A sad-looking waiter shuffled in, took our orders and shuffled out. The men who had previously been sitting in the shed outside came in and sat at a table nearby. Somehow Amina seemed to have lost her tongue, and I did not want to press her. I was still smarting at the fact that in a place like Lagos women

18

who went to a hotel restaurant to have lunch should be regarded as 'business women'. Then the men's voices floated over. They were speaking in Yoruba and did not know that we were Lagos Yoruba too. Our outfits were made in the East, so they took it for granted that we were either Easterners or Ghanaian women.

'Those are some of them,' nodded one man with a conspiratorial wink.

'I know, don't look. These women are so desperate and shameless these days that they have to hawk their wares during the day. These are the expensive ones so they come to expensive places like this one.'

'Why should I pay so much for them when I can get a beautiful, young Ghanaian chick at Ajegunle for less than a bowl of soup?' They all laughed at this crude joke, forgetting that some desperate Nigerian girls were doing the same thing in many parts of the world. Then the same man continued, 'I spent the night here. And that woman Ali gave me, I did not give her a moment's peace.'

'How much did she charge then?' asked another one, laughing.

'I did not wait to find out. She was too young, and did not have the courage to demand her rights, so I did not give her a single kobo. That will teach her to stay at home.'

'Left to me these prostitutes would never make a living. What joy do people derive from jumping up and down on another human being,' the skinniest and the weakiest looking among them added.

I was by this time seething with anger and Amina started to mouth, 'Auntie, let's go. They will think we are one of them.'

So I raised my voice and said in Yoruba, 'I am not one of them and I am here to buy lunch as I promised. No silly talk from uncultivated men is going to force us to go away. For your information, I am a professor of English and this is my sister-in-law . . .'

I did not have to finish my sentence. The confused men got up and some of them walked out of the restaurant almost without the use of their eyes, knocking against this and that in their hurry to get out.

'Oh Auntie Bintu!' Amina now relaxed again. 'They are men, that is the only thing they can think of. Forget about it. You see, few women can afford to come and spend forty naira on an ordinary lunch, when they knew that they could cook it at the fraction of that price at home. It is not so common for us — only kept women with real bottom power or top been-tos can afford it. You are a been-to, but you wear our costume, so you can't blame the men. It is not their fault.'

'Then is it the fault of the women?'

Our forty naira order started to arrive, and Amina's eyes were like saucers. As she munched and drank, and enjoyed herself, she told me the story of the Ubakanma family. Sometimes she called them Ubaks, depending on how strong the hold the mild wine was getting on her. But one thing I knew that my sister-in-law learnt that day was this — sometimes housewives too need to go out and enjoy food cooked by somebody else, without having to worry about the price or the washing up. I wish a lot of our men would realise this, instead of just buying presents in the form of cloth, all the time. It is said that the way to a man's heart is through his belly, and I'm sure the same goes for women, especially those tied to their homes all day, year in year out, with strings of children to raise.

3 What's in a name?

'You know, Auntie Bintu, it is true when people say that we name a new-born child according to the conditions in the family during its birth.'

I nodded, not wanting to interrupt Amina's flow of words.

'Not only is it true, but many a time we behave according to the hope and expectation our people have in naming us. I remember, when I was at school, I heard people saying that the boys the Ibos named Adolphus were usually violent. So I think Ubakanma's fate was due to his family name. Ubakanma. You know what the name means?'

'I don't, but I know it's not a Yoruba name. It sounds Iboish and I wouldn't be surprised if you knew, knowing the way you are with languages.'

'I can't help it. You know what Lagos is. As children we had friends from Hausaland, the Lemonu family, and across our road lived our Togolese neighbours the Folis, and we had Ibos, the Ezes, down the road. My brother knew the Ubakanmas through the Ezes. They all used to play football together at Odan, so I too came to know the family and picked up a few words of Ibo. Not just a few words, I do really understand what they say, but you know, not having lived in Iboland, my accent cannot be right. So though I understand it, yet I am too shy to speak it.'

'But you do speak Hausa,' I said rather unfeelingly before I could stop myself, knowing how close Ramonu and my sister-in-law had been before she married Nurudeen, my brother. I checked myself in time and apologised. But my sister-in-law Amina was too drunk with freedom and happiness to take offence.

She waved her bangled hands in the air and expanded airily, 'Auntie Bintu, all those things happened in the past. I have washed Ramonu out of my system, and the pain about him has now dulled. But I speak Hausa, yes.'

'So what does Ubakanma mean and what has it to do with the people in the story you are going to tell me?'

'Well it was like this Auntie Bintu, the story is about the Ubakanma family. The name literally means, "It is better for us to be many". So I think Mr Ubakanma senior went through his life wanting to be many. But though he strove and strove to have a compound filled with children and wives, fate denied his wish and because he decided to force his fate, or what they call their *Chi* and we call *Eleda* it all ended in a terrible tragedy ...'

We were both silent as we watched the serving girl bring in our hot pounded yam and rich *efo* soup. They were both piping hot, and this forced my sister-in-law to say, 'I keep meaning to cook pounded yam one day, but the trouble of going through the motions is always too much. To think that in the old days, we ate it a lot. Now it is a great luxury.'

'In the old days most of us lived in compounds where you stood the *odo* and pounded away. Now we live in flats. What would happen to the people downstairs if you pounded *odo* over their heads every day? Or are you thinking of the machine-pounded yam? I don't know if it tastes the same.'

'Yes, that is true.' Amina dug her hand into the mound of pounded yam. 'You see,' she said as she swallowed, 'Ubakanma went to the UK in the late forties, a very, very long time ago. And there, while Madam Ubakanma was training as a nurse, they met. They say that it used to be very, very lonely for African students in those days and that was why many of the men came back with white wives. But funnily enough most of those early marriages really worked. The women, those who returned with their husbands, stayed, didn't they Auntie Bintu?'

'Yes, Amina those marriages worked because those were the days before Independence when our people thought that there was something special about Europeans. Also in those days, if you married white you got a good job here in Nigeria, because the British people did not want their daughters to suffer,' I explained.

'But those men, did they not marry many wives in those days?' Amina asked.

'If one married a white woman, it was most uncommon for him to look for another wife. That's one of the reasons why mothers-in-law still do not like their sons marrying white. But Amina, did Ubakanma marry white?'

'No, no, Ubaks did not marry white. He was studying Economics at London University and went to that place where our students always go to take their photos with bewitched pigeons standing all over them. Eh, eh, what's the name of the place again, it's long . . .'

24

'I know, it's Trafalgar Square. And those pigeons are not bewitched you know.'

'Then why don't they fly away when they see people instead of standing still on people's heads and arms and allowing their photos to be taken?'

'That, Amina, is because they are now so used to people, and people are kind to them.'

'People kind to pigeons!' Amina burst out laughing. I had to laugh too because I could guess what she was going to come out with.

'Can you imagine pigeons flying about like that at Tinubu Square?' We both laughed so much that we almost choked. Amina went on, 'You know our neighbour's cat was eaten the other day? I always told her it was silly to keep cats where so many people have no jobs and can't afford to buy good meat. Can you imagine what would have happened if she had kept pigeons instead? Anyway Ubakanma met Maria when she came to Trafalgar Square with her colleagues. She was a nurse and she looked very attractive in her nurse's uniform. She is still a beautiful woman. But because she took so long finishing her teacher training before she decided to be a nurse, she was already in her early thirties when she met Ubakanma. Ubaks, as my oldest brother used to call him, was very handsome and very clever. You know how those Ibos worshipped education. He stopped playing with my brother when they were both in their late teens. Then, as my brother was busy looking for a short cut through life, Ubaks was working hard at his studies.'

'Ah, ah, wait a minute Amina. How many children did your father have — you were many weren't you and when your mother left your father, did your father not threaten to remove your brother from school?'

'No, Father did not, but life was tough for us. With Mother gone and Father's new wife, and so many of us — and as for our neighbours the Lemonus, I think they had about twenty children.'

'And how many children did the Ubakanmas have?'

'Only Ubaks and his sister, whom we seldom saw. She was soon whisked to Queen's College. She was the first lady I ever met who attended that posh school in those days. But this story, Auntie Bintu, is about her brother and his wife Maria. They soon got married over there in the United Kingdom. The husband got a good job in our Embassy in London and soon they had their first son Osita. Life was very sweet for them because, Auntie Bintu, despite the cold weather over there in England they had a big house and servants ...'

'Wait a minute, Amina this must be around or after our Independence in 1960 because Ubaks could not have got a job in the Embassy around that time.'

'Auntie Bintu, this was the way I heard it. That he worked for the then Foreign Office — you know the token office we had in London — because did not those Europeans know that in a few years we would be getting our Independence anyway?'

'Yes,' I nodded. There was a Nigerian Office which later became our Embassy in London.

'But though Ubaks wanted many more sons and daughters after Osita, none came. And Maria was beautiful and a good hostess, and so Ubaks learnt to live like a European, with just one baby son and a beautiful wife and hostess.'

'Is that bad Amina?'

'No, I don't think it's bad Auntie Bintu, only we don't do things like that. Suppose that son died, what would happen? That is why it is good, Auntie Bintu, to have at least four or five children, because you know what we Yorubas say, that the person who is buried by his children is the one with children. If one is unfortunate enough to bury his only child, then that person is childless.'

'In other words one must pray to be buried by one's children, and not the other way round.'

'Exactly, Auntie Bintu.'

'Amina, lift your wine glass and let's toast or pray to that.'

'May our children mourn and bury us.'

'Amiiiii Amiii, big big Amiii.'

Amina and I clicked our glasses together and drained the contents. Amina's eyes started to sparkle and for once I was a little concerned in case she got too drunk to drive the short distance home. Lagos traffic was impossible enough for a driver with a clear head to say nothing of someone whose vision was blurred with much wine. I looked at our bottle of wine and knew that we had drunk it all, so we had to wait, and I had to encourage her to tell me the story slowly over coffee. Hopefully by the time she came to the end of the Ubakanma story, the effect of the wine would have worn off.

'So life was sweet for the Ubakanmas in England,' I probed.

'Oh yes, and they were so happy that the husband did not even realise that his Maria had failed him by giving him only one son, Osita. A few years later it was time for them to go home. All the Ubakanma family went to the airport to welcome their son and his beautiful wife. The family was so happy at seeing them that Mrs Ubaks Senior danced all the way home from the airport.'

'Oh, Aminotu, how could an old woman dance all the way from the old Ikeja airport to Isale Eko? Exaggeration, exaggeration!'

Amina laughed. 'Well, you know Auntie Bintu, she was so delirious with happiness all the way. And when they got home, there were parties and parties of welcome that went on for days and days. My brother was invited to one of them because he was Charles Ubaka's friend before he went to England and became a very rich man.

'I lost contact with them when I married Nurudeen, your brother, and I think they moved away. When I say "they", Auntie Bintu, I mean Charles and "the Ubakanmas are going to be many soon". I thought that Maria did not want many children when they were in England because they say it costs a great deal of money to raise one over there. Then, much later, I thought she wanted to settle in her new job first, because I know that with a man like Ubakanma she was expected to have a house full of children. However, as time went on and she did not have any more, I said well, that probably was how Allah wanted it.'

We watched wordlessly as a serving man hovered over another customer at the other end of the eating room. I mouthed the name 'Ubakanma', which means the large family is better, and sighed. What a lot to expect from a young family! Fate had really dealt unfairly with Charles when he found himself saddled with such a name and, by one of those unhappy strokes Providence deals out to the innocent, only able to have one son with his wife, Maria. The young serving man moved away and I looked at Amina's sweaty face and asked, 'So how come you saw them again after so many years?'

4 The market stalls

'It's a small world, Auntie Bintu.'

'Yes I know.' I nodded like a lizard in my attempt to urge Amina on.

'If you walk into Jankara market in Lagos, and you make your way towards the sea, you'll come to the plate sellers. If you look closely at these women you notice that somehow they look alike, and they have monopolised the trade.'

'I know this, Amina, because my mother was one of them. They all came from the Badagry area. And don't they all look heavy, dark, and very, very feminine? You remember how my mother used to decorate her knees with beads and how fond she used to be of maize and anything made of maize? Oh those women, how hard they worked.'

'Right, Auntie Bintu. A woman's work is never done. Don't we still work from morning till night and that is never enough for our existence. We are expected to do all that and then to fill our husband's house with children as well.'

'And in most cases bring up those children for our husbands whilst in the end they bear his name.'

'What a rotten deal! But Auntie, as I was saying, the senior Mrs Ubakanma came from Badagry too. I saw her when I went to the stall to see our Big Mother, your mother, and there she was. She did not remember who I was, and I had to reintroduce myself to her. Looking back now, I still don't think she remembered me well, but the fact that I am married to Nurudeen, the son of a friend and her market neighbour was enough for her, so she started to call me "daughter". It was then that I caught up with their story. But soon after that they retired, and our mother retired too. The senior Ubakanma went back to the East, I think around Enuga or Onitsha. I am not sure where exactly the father came from, but one thing I am sure of was that he came from Iboland.

'So her son Charles and Maria lived on happily in Lagos. Then suddenly, Charles started to go on some mysterious tours for his job. He would breeze in and would say nicely to Maria, "Sorry, darling, but this weekend I shall be away and will be back on Monday in time for work in the office." And if Maria should say, "But, darling Charles, surely they can allow you to have the weekends free, at least for your family?" he would snap and march out of the house taking their driver with him. So Maria learnt to be quiet.

'And poor Maria did not just accept the fact that she could not fill Charles Ubakanma's house with children, she did everything she could about it. They said that despite all her education and sophistication she went to Celesial Apostolic Faith . . .'

'No, she did not!' I cried, as the image of men dancing in white robes by the beach and gibbering about in strange tongues which they claimed were the languages of the Holy Prophets came into my mind. I knew that if you allowed some of the *Wolis* to penetrate into your family, they could actually control your private lives. In my mind's eyes I could not see Charles Ubakanma fitting into that mould of men who would submit to such degredations. But then in Nigeria, where would people not go and what would they not do to have children of their own? In fact most people feel that you are here simply to produce children, and if you failed on that score, you have failed to justify your life. It does not matter what you might have achieved in other fields. This is even more so for women.

'No, I know what you are thinking, Auntie Bintu. When the *Woli* said that Charles should come and plant a child into Maria in front of their altar, Maria stopped going.'

We both burst out laughing. Whatever would these *Woli* prophets not do to desperate people! And I sometimes wonder if such recommendations could be found in the Holy Scriptures.

'I studied the Bible when I was little, even though I am a Muslim. But I don't think the Bible said that one must sleep with one's wife in front of the altar?'

'Well when a human is desperate for one thing, little insults can pile on top of his desperation unless he is clever enough to call a stop at any point. But, Auntie Bintu, you have heard of that tribe in eastern Africa? They do something like that but they call it "fertility rites".'

'Oh Amina, you do read and hear so many things. How did you hear about that?'

'I did not read about it, I saw it on television. The women collect money and goats and give things to the men to eat and drink, and then the men are asked to bless the women in return. And after the ceremony they give the women babies, and if one of the women becomes pregnant, then it has been a good fertility rite. I thought it was awful but the *Wolis* of some of the Cherubim and Seraphims have now included similar rights in their worship to calm the desperate barren women.'

We were quiet and then thought for a while. Then I said, 'Look Amina, these vagaries are not just a speciality of Nigeria. Most religions are like that. For example we Nigerian Muslims are not as fanatic as our brothers and sisters in Iran and Iraq, and though most Pakistanis are Muslims, I have not seen many with several wives like the men have in Nigeria.'

'Maybe they are too poor to have many wives?' Amina said, her bulging eyes looking into the distance.

'Maybe so,' I replied, agreeing and at the same time wondering whether we would have wished our men poor, simply to have just us alone and not look at other women. I thought about this for a while but, since I could find no answer, I urged Amina on.

'So did Maria take any more steps about her barrenness, when she did not have the courage to tell her husband that she had been seeing a *Woli*?'

'Yes, she did. Being a nurse she went to this doctor and that doctor they did on her all the D and Cs they could, but she did not conceive. And after a while the poor but very beautiful woman just accepted it. She noticed one thing though, and that was that her husband became monosyllabic with her. Then suddenly that horrible civil war came.'

'Which civil war, Amina?'

'Oh Auntie, how many civil wars have we had — we only had one, the Biafran war. That year was terrible. We all suffered, but I think the life of the average Ibo man was totally disrupted. For a while Maria and Charles went on with their jobs, until many Ibo people started to fear for their lives. They had reason to be frightened, because they said that some of them started to disappear without trace. So Charles and Maria Ubakanma left Lagos and went back to their village in Iboland. Their Big Mother too, though not originally from Iboland, went with her family. It was a rotten war, as many people had started intermarrying before then. Suddenly you saw a family divided ... I am Ibo, you are Hausa and you're this and that — all in the same family; it was a nightmare, I can tell you. But the Big Mother from Badagry had accepted her husband's tribe and went with them. In fact the old couple went home first, before Maria and Charles decided to follow, years later because of the war.'

'That war was not only a bad thing, it was unfair to many people. Did you not say that Charles was born in Lagos?'

'Yes,' Amina nodded. 'He was a pure Lagosian, just like you and I, but you know that here if your grandparents came from Iboland, you are always Ibo, even though you and your parents were born in a place like Lagos. You know, Auntie Bintu, maybe when we are as rich as the Americans we won't be that finicky about this or that tribe.'

'That will be the day, that will be the day,' I said as I lifted my hands in mock prayer.

'You may laugh Auntie Bintu, but I don't think that day is too far off. Don't many of our young people who were born in Europe just marry any Nigerian, without bothering about their tribe? The parents of such students are too happy that their children have married a black person, and a Nigerian for that matter, to start worrying about tribes. I think it will happen. Why we worry about this tribe or that tribe is because of poverty and those silly politicians. After all didn't the Big Ubakanma Mother come from Badagry and end up in Iboland, and didn't Ramonu's father come from the North and aren't all his offspring now Lagosians?'

As I did not want to be unnecessarily pessimistic I agreed with Amina, and prayed that soon all Nigerian sons and daughters would touch their hearts when the Nigerian National Anthem was sung instead of beating their tribal war drums.

5 Civilisation

'When Maria and Charles arrived in their parents' town, Ibusa, it was evening. The day's terrible heat had given way to a caressing evening, one of those rare evenings which are the great bounties of our tropical weather. Normally people arrived from Lagos in this part of the country in the early mornings, having travelled by night, but they no longer did this because those civil war days were dangerous days especially for an Ibo family going home. Charles and Maria and their handsome thirteen-year-old son Osita had to weave around the main road. Sometimes for safety they would avoid driving near a popular route for miles and miles and many a time Charles and his cousin Umunna, who was travelling with them, would take out cutlasses and cut their way through the bush. It was a good thing that the cousin knew the lay of the country so well for, unlike his cousin Charles, he had received all his education in Nigeria. So when eventually they sighted Agbor, and heard people speaking in Ibo, they sighed with relief. And in less than two hours they were speeding along the road from Asaba to Ibusa. The soldiers had not reached those parts by then, and it was refreshing to come across people who still knew only the rumours of the war and had not actually seen it.

'Maria and Charles were not happy to leave their

jobs in Lagos, and did not think that Osita having to leave his school, King's College, would do the lad any good. But knowing that many of their Ibo friends had lost their lives in an attempt to save their jobs and living standards in the big towns, they counted themselves lucky. At least they had their lives and it would give Osita and Maria an opportunity to get to know Charles' parents better, especially as the old man had now taken a title. He was now an Obi.

' "Oh good old Ibusa, you are like a mother who welcomes all your children every time they get into trouble in those foreign places. How I wish I never had to leave you, never had to go to places where people say you're this or you're that," Charles cried.

' "I used to feel like that in England, and I would then control myself and say that when we returned home to Nigeria all that kind of labelling would be over. Now look at us fleeing from one part of the country to another simply because our grandparents were born here. What a lot of bother we cause each other." Maria put in.

' "If we are staying here, we will choke ourselves up. Our present trouble is caused by greed, but it is twenty times better than colonial times, at least we now rule ourselves," Umunna who had never left Nigeria said wisely.

' "Pooh some ruling, some government," Charles said in derision.

' "Hmm. I'm sure it will be all right some day, and we'll all go back to our jobs and live in harmony as we used to before the beginning of all this. But just look at this beautiful scenery. Isn't Ibusa beautiful?"

' "I know what you mean Maria, I always have this feeling every time I travel this road. I sometimes wish my job at the Secretariat was nearer home. This forest gives one a sense of secret peace, which is indescribable."

'Maria laughed here and remarked uneasily, "But Charles you've only been home once or twice in these past eight years, now you talk as if you visit Ibusa often."

'Auntie Bintu, when Maria made this observation, the silence that fell in that car was like a solid rock that wedged itself among the previously happy and light-hearted passengers. Charles started to concentrate unnecessarily on his driving, and as for that cousin Umunna he began to look out of the car window intently as if his life depended on it.

' "Have I said something wrong?" Maria asked in all innocence, but getting no answer from the two men, she shrugged the incident off as one of those eccentricities men often indulge in.

'The Big Mother saw them first and she shouted and danced for joy with her ample arms open in welcome. Those were anxious days for the old people at home, because bad news was coming fast. So if you had a relative outside the Iboland, you kept praying for their safety. And when they eventually arrived home, and well, the joy was always too big for people to contain.

'To see the way that the Big Mother behaved people say you would have thought that she had been born in that very village. She knew the people really well, and she understood their language and customs — so much so that, when her husband was made an Obi, she had the string of the Obi's wife tied around her ankle without any objection from anybody.'

'How long ago did that Mamma from Badagry

marry into this Ibusa family?' I asked, interrupting Amina.

'I am not quite sure but they had Charles and he was then nearly forty, if not more.'

'Well, Amina, forty years is a long time to be married. After all those years, I'd be surprised if she ever thought about the Badagry of her youth, which would have changed beyond her recognition anyway.'

Amina gulped a glass of water and nodded. 'We women are sometimes like cattle, we just follow whoever paid for us, and tend to forget our original parents.'

'Well, that's the way it has always been. The Koran said we must be obedient to our husbands, and we must leave our original parents . . .'

'Raw deal, why can't men leave their parents for us?' Amina asked, her eyes dancing in mischief.

'They do in some foreign countries where people regard marriage partners as equal. If the wife is richer or has a better job the whole family could go with her and if the husband is richer, the arrangements could be other way.'

'But Auntie Bintu, how would such a man feel? If he had to live off his wife? Would he be obedient to her as we are to our husbands just because they control the purse?'

'Some of those men could be very masterful and really wicked. In some English novels I have read, they would even plot the death of that wife so that they could take all her money and marry a serving maid.'

'Ah, that is very bad. But why do they have to kill the rich wife in order to marry a poor girl?'

'Because Amina, there they practise monogamy,

one man one wife. If a man longed for another woman or slept with her, the wife could sue for divorce.'

'Hmmm,' sighed Amina, 'maybe there is something in polygamy after all.'

'Polygamy has its good aspects, especially when people are getting on. When they are young and tempers are hot, many women may not like it, but when they grow older they find that they can enjoy the company of another woman, and their large compound family. But Amina, what happened to Maria and Charles when they arrived in Ibusa?'

'Oh them, I almost forget I was telling you their story. Well, when they got there, they were shown their room and they were allowed to rest for the first night. The following morning all their relatives came to visit them. The Obi was sitting on his usual stool almost like someone holding council because his younger relatives were always coming to him to settle this case or that or to borrow some money. But the fact that Charles and his family had arrived safe and well from Lagos gave them all the opportunity they wanted to visit the Obi, or so Maria thought.

'Maria, innocently playing the beautiful and sophisticated wife from Lagos, tidied herself, put on a wrapper of very nice George material and came into the compound to greet the Obi.

' "You slept well my daughter?" the Obi asked solicitously.

' "Yes, Obi, but I would like to go and see my parents at Umuodafe to tell them that we are back. My parents must be wondering about us."

'The Big Mother heard this and left the compound abruptly. Maria noticed how tense everybody was, but she thought it was her imagination.

40

' "I have a few words to tell you, my beautiful wife Maria. Please sit down and I shall come to you by and by. There is plenty of time for your parents, because no one knows when this war is going to end."

' "You're very right, Obi."

'Maria went back into the house and brought out some nice kolanuts for the Obi to pray with. She called her son Osita and told him to wash them properly. The boy soon returned with the washed kolanuts and Maria presented them to the Obi.

' "Ah daughter, thank you. Were you taking them all to your parents?" he asked in joke, looking up at Maria.

' "No Father, I bought them for you specially."

' "Good answer. Then let us use them in praying for your *Chi* and for the Ubakanma compound."

'The Obi took the kolanuts and started to pray for the usual good fortune and health and Maria noticed that he was unnecessarily dwelling on the family name Ubakanma, the crowd is better and safer and this should be desired rather than compound or family with one child. "I hope you have more sons and daughters. Osita is all right but he wants more brothers and sisters. What have you been doing Maria, all these fourteen years, not to present us with another child? How do you think your husband must feel . . ."

'Then there was a slight rustle near the doorway leading from the Obi's compound. Maria looked up and saw the Big Ubakanma mother dragging an unwilling boy with her. "Come on, come on, Afam, come and see the rest of your family, your brother Osita and your Big Mother Maria."

'The Obi got up in anger and shouted at his wife.

"Why, woman, do you have to do it this way? Charles promised to tell her gently in his own good time. You know how these people who have been abroad behave. They have different ways."

'Charles, who heard raised voices, left their room and came into the compound. "Mother, Mother what are you doing?" he cried.

'The Big Mother disregarded both men. She gripped the wriggling boy and marched him up to Maria and said, "This is your second son, Afam, and he's got a little sister still on her mother's back. Here take him, he's your husband's son."

'Maria looked out of the compound and saw a nice looking young woman with a baby on her back. The mother of Afam, no doubt. She turned round and looked at Charles, and her mouth formed his name.

'Charles was obviously worried and his eyes behind his silver-rimmed glasses were red with agitation. He walked up quickly to Maria and said, "I can explain, give me time to explain everything, please Maria."

'Maria was quick to note that the compound seemed suddenly filled with people who were there to see her break down and cry "Judas" to Charles. She was determined to give them nothing to dance about. She only asked Charles quietly, "Is Afam your son?"

'Charles nodded and began to say that he could explain how it happened.

'Maria brushed his excuses aside and called, "Osita, Osita, take your little brother to the stream and give him a bath. Put some of those shirts that are too small for you on him. I am going to see my parents, at Umuodafe."

'With that Maria left the compound, her head high,

her George cloth sweeping the floor and her shiny toenails peeping out of the white sandals she wore.

'The Big Mother, now deprived of all the drama she had expected, and worked herself up for, hissed and spat, "Hmmm, so this is civilisation."

6 Visit to Maria's mother

'Maria, until that mid-morning, had not realised how light one's feet could be when one's heart was fuelled by sorrow caused by betrayal. To think that Charles, who had courted and married her in a big city like London, could allow himself to stoop this low, simply because he wanted to live up to his surname, Ubakanma — the crowd is better. She walked lightly, tripping over this shrub and over that bush, her heart pounding and her mouth tasting bitter. When she reached the little bush that separated her village from that of Umueze, where her husband's grandparents came from, she shouted to the dark bush, "Oh my God, why do you punish women like myself so?" The bush did not answer her back, because the bush, though it had been there for generations, could find no answer either. Only the ever-busy birds and the sounds of invisible animals could be heard. She took the edge of her expensive George waist *lappa* and wiped away her hot tears. She was a Christian who always believed that God would never allow any of his creatures to be tempted more than they could bear. With that as a temporary consolation, she walked to her parents' place in Umuodafe.

'She turned from the *Owele* — the women's bush — right into her father's compound. She had taken this route specially because as she was leaving she had heard Charles calling her to wait because he was going to take her to her parents' by car. What a hypocrite Charles was turning out to be! Going to her parents via the *Owele* meant that her husband could not follow her. The bush path was too narrow for his Mercedes, and most women would wonder what a man like Charles was doing taking that particular path.

'When she turned into her own village, she could not escape her relatives. The ever-present Ojinma and his mother Ngbolie were there sitting as usual outside their house. As always they were happy to see her and shouted their greeting.

' "Welcome back, my daughter and my husband!" Ngbolie, although she was very old, gave every child born in Umuodafe his or her due respect. She knew though that by greeting people so nicely, they would be bound to give her a naira or two to buy her daily ration of *Otaba* tobacco. She smoked so much pipe tobacco that one could not help wondering whether her lungs and nostrils would not be like a chimney. Ngbolie must have been about ninety at this time.'

'So what did Maria do to Ngbolie, then?'

'Oh, Maria walked up to her and gave her a naira and another to Ngbolie's son Ojinma who protested violently because he, being a man, wanted more than one naira. So Maria had to give him two naira. Then he asked her to kneel down, and blessed her with the piece of kolanut he was holding. Again Ojinma had to ask her *Chi* to give her more children because she was not too old yet. "What are you doing there, you the *Chi* of this our beautiful daughter? Isn't it time she should be rocking another child to and fro? Why should you be satisfied to give her only one son? That

45

one son will stay and be a big man, but he needs a subordinate, because *Azubike* — our backers — are our strength. A single son's standing is very shaky. But with another, younger brother, then he stands firmly and solidly like the *ukwa* tree. So go in peace, daughter, your *Chi* will hear your prayers, and thank you for the money you gave your old relatives. The Obi Uwunno, your father, is waiting for you. We have heard what they did to you a few minutes ago at Umueze. Go in peace."

'In her father's compound her mother was waiting for her again with arms open in welcome. "Come in, good daughter; just come in."

'Obi Uwunno, who had not been very well, got up on seeing his daughter, Maria. He blessed her anew and would not drink any alcohol because of his illness, but accepted the kolanut she gave to him.

'Maria poured her heart out to her parents who listened to her without interruption until she came to the very end.

' "And what did you do when Madam Ubakanma presented to you the little boy Afam?" her father asked.

' "I welcomed him with open arms, Father. What else is there for me to do?" Maria cried tearfully.

' "And that is why God is going to bless you for it. You see your husband is right. One person cannot make a crowd. Your son needs a brother. In future you'll see that Afam is his greatest friend — and not just a friend but an ally, the type he would not be able to find anywhere else. And Maria, my daughter, when your husband comes to apologise to you, listen to him. He is a nice man. We knew he had been coming to Ibusa to see that girl Obioma, and we heard when

Afam was born, but it was a hard truth, which we did not have the heart to tell you. We know you see things differently, but here it is a man's world. If he had not been able to give you a child, you would have been expected to stay with him or have a man friend and bear a son in his name. You would not be expected to leave him. He is not casting you aside. The reason that he did not tell you about it is because he fears and respects you," her mother said.

' "Pooh, some respect," Obi Uwenno taunted. "Those Europeans have unmanned most of our men. What's bad in a man taking another woman and telling his wife? You are my daughter, Maria, and I sympathise, but if Charles were my son, I would have done the same thing. But the way you reacted . . . well that is expected of my daughter anyway. When this horrible war is over take the child to Lagos with you and give him the same type of education you are now giving Osita, so that in future there will be no jealousy between brothers."

'Towards evening Charles came for Maria, and he apologised all the way home. Maria was quiet, but she knew what she was going to do. And in the dark hours when they were alone she said, "Charles, I understand you could not help the pressure your family put you under. That is all right. But you must appreciate the fact that though my son Osita, God bless him, is your first son, he will be out-numbered. So, if you don't mind, I will keep my income separate from now on, so that my son can inherit my things. I will help you look after your new children, but not with my money. And another thing, that woman is not coming to live with us in Lagos. You met her here, so she is your Ibusa wife. That is all I have to say."

'Charles jumped up in bed. "But Maria, your income provides for almost half the expenses we run in this household. If you keep it all to yourself our living standard will be much lower. We will have to send at least one of our servants away and you know that Osita's education costs a great deal. You know that I plan to send him abroad earlier than necessary because of this stupid war. If you withhold your income your son Osita too will suffer."

' "Ah, Charles, one minute Osita is our son, next minute he is 'my son Osita'. Don't worry about his education. I will pay for it all. What else is there for me to live for?" Maria began to cry and Charles marched about the room in great anger, yet Maria was determined.

'Well, that went on for almost a year, but Maria made sure her son was sent to a posh private school in England. She had friends there, you see, and those friends helped her by looking after him during the holidays. She did not allow Osita to come home for a long time, not even when he was admitted to a university hospital to be trained as a doctor. Maria would go to England every summer to see her son and to have a rest, whilst Charles went on doing his work.'

'But Amina, did their living standard go down when they returned to Lagos when the war was over?'

'Oh yes, Auntie Bintu, what did you expect? Maria was already a qualified nursing sister at the time and earning as much as any doctor. So she learned how to drive and bought her own car instead of sharing the Mercedes with her husband. The driver had to go because Charles insisted on keeping the Mercedes. But they had only one maid of all works — you know

48

Auntie Bintu, a house-maid instead of a steward, gardener and the rest of them.'

'I think I know what you mean, Amina. Women like Maria could be financially powerful in their families.'

'But that is true, Auntie Bintu. Many of our people abroad were sent there by their mothers and these are facts that are never noised about. An intelligent woman can really reap a lot from a polygamous home because she is not compelled to help her husband. If he is rich enough to keep another woman, then he is rich enough to keep her and cater for all her needs, so he has no right to ask his first wife what she does with the money she earns.'

'That is also true, Amina. But in Maria's case she paid for their son's expensive education.'

'Because she wanted to, not because she had to. Charles would not have been able to afford such a sophisticated life for their son, not with Afam and his little sister, Nneka, and their mother Obioma, who could not read or write but sold peppers in Ibusa market. But he would have still have received a good education nevertheless.

'In any case all that was still in the future. Meanwhile, that horrid Nigerian civil war continued.

7 *Afam is established*

'Maria watched helplessly as the marriage between her and Charles became completely invaded by his parents, then gradually by Afam's mother. Her name was Obioma. Obioma was beautiful in a natural way, not the sophisticated way in which Maria was beautiful. To Obioma that civil war was a blessing, because it brought the father of her children home to Ibusa.

'She had threatened many times to go to Lagos herself and break the news to Maria, but let's face it, Auntie Bintu, Afam was then a chubby five-year-old boy and his sister was almost two. However illiterate Obioma was, no woman deserves to be treated like that.'

'Like what, Amina? Did she not know that Charles was married before she agreed to be his second wife?'

'Of course the poor girl knew, but, like all second and third wives, she expected to be invited into the family home once she had had a boy. She had Afam, but Charles still preferred to visit her two or three times a year or so. And remember, Auntie Bintu, this was a woman who was still around twenty-four or twenty-five years of age. I think she accepted the arrangement because of the money in Ubakanma's family and also because of Big Mother's kindness. She treated Obioma like her very own daughter, so this made it impossible for the girl to be lonely or to feel deprived of her husband's affection.'

'Amina, did you say her husband?'

Amina nodded vigorously like a fallen lizard. 'Yes Auntie Bintu, all those trips which Maria thought were official business were visits to Ibusa to arrange the marriage settlement on Obioma.'

'Then I don't care what you say about Charles, he was a liar,' I spat in anger. 'Maria at least deserved to be told the truth.'

Amina laughed, really amused at what she considered my naivety, 'Auntie Bintu, you know your trouble — you have never belonged to a large family or lived in a polygamous one. If you had you'd know that "truth is not always the best policy". We all tell lies to protect the people we love. You can see a young person who has been badly wounded and who you know will probably die and tell her what you know. On the other hand you can cheer her up and tell her to hurry up and get better, and not tell her that she is going to die. Or if a woman has been unfaithful to her husband once, but then the marriage became better, she would be stupid to go and start confessing to her husband, because that kind of truth is a selfish truth, she probably wants her husband to carry her guilt. So, Auntie Bintu, if you think about it you'll know that people tell lies in most cases for good reasons. Many truths are better not told.'

My sister-in-law Amina always amazed me. That laughing, puffy-cheeked, obviously extrovert woman did a great deal of thinking by her sink in Festac village, Lagos. So, rather than expose my ignorance about a matter I had not given much thought, I said airily, 'Well, that is an academic topic.'

'What's that Auntie Bintu?'

'I mean that it's a matter of opinion. I'd hate to be found out if I lied.'

'But, Auntie Bintu, if you are found out, that makes you even more human. For let's face it, who wants to stay with somebody who is always right, always pure and always speaks the truth. Ow, a person like that would give me a pain. He would be like Allah himself. Try and find me such person, Auntie Bintu.' Amina laughed and I joined in for I did not have the courage to touch my heart and say, 'Here is one sitting in front of you', because she knew that we always tell our relatives what they want to hear. I wouldn't, for example, dare tell the old lady next door to them the actual date of my leaving for London, otherwise she would buy all the foodstuff she could for her son who lives in Newcastle. I have tried several times to tell her that England may not be as big as Nigeria, but that people have towns over there and that London is too far from Newcastle for me to carry a pawpaw, yam or black eye beans. Her son was already overfed in England anyway. So in a way Amina had a point.

'At length, though, Charles could not disguise his desire for Obioma?' I prompted her.

'You're right, Auntie, and Maria, though she shared the same room with her husband, found that many a night Charles was not there. Charles used the fact that Maria had refused to contribute to the household budget as an excuse. So whilst Charles concentrated on Obioma, Maria concentrated on Osita. As I said, it was at this time that Osita left for the United Kingdom. The war was coming to an end then and it looked as if the Ibos might all be going back to their old jobs. Maria used that opportunity to come to the UK with her son. She did it this way to avoid having to make the decision about Afam and his mother Obioma.

'When Maria came to London she consulted with many specialists but the treatment recommended was expensive and not only that, she would need Charles with her most of the time to do things like temperature charts and banking his sperm and all the rubbishy things people in Europe do to have a child.'

'Amina they are not rubbishy and they do work. Many white people have had what they now call test-tube babies and the babies are quite normal.'

'Auntie Bintu, this was before the age of test-tube babies. But can you imagine a man of Charles Ubakanma's standing allowing himself to be messed up like that simply because his wife could not conceive? If his mother should know about it, it would kill her, Auntie Bintu, it would.'

'Well, his mother need not know and greater men have subjected themselves to such tests you know. I am sure Charles would have done it when they were here.'

'Ah, Auntie Bintu, you are now agreeing with me about telling the truth. If they were still there they could have done it without telling the old lady. They would have just told her that they had had a child normally if it had worked. But Maria could not get Charles to London and she had to give it all up.

'She looked well, trim and groomed the day she arrived in Lagos. Charles came to meet her, much to her surprise, because even though she had had her way with her money and there was the added joy of knowing that her job was secure, she did not know what to expect. She had wondered whether Charles would give up completely their former living standards and go native by bringing Obioma to Lagos. So as he kissed and admired her physically, her heart palpitated, and she did not wish to ask any questions.

'Their apartment at Ikoyi was clean but bare. Most of their things had either been stolen or left in Ibusa. Then Charles poured them a drink and, as neighbours came to welcome her, she heard a little boy's voice calling "Mummy, Mummy, welcome back. What did you bring for me?"

'With this Afam dashed into the room with his hair sweaty and wearing clammy shorts. He had been playing football with his friends in the open spaces at Ikoyi. Maria, thus taken unawares, opened her arms and welcomed the boy. She looked over his head at Charles and the anger and restraint between husband and wife seemed to evaporate. And for the first time Maria thought that he must have suffered too, trying to please her and his mother — two women tearing him apart.

' "Oh yes, I bought you some nice clothes and your brother Osita sent his love and some toys."

' "Toys, toys, where are they? What are they?"

' "Eh, eh, Afam, go out and play now, your mother has just returned and she is very tired. Come on, go on out."

'But there and then Afam displayed the kind of stubbornness Maria and Charles did not see in their gentle boy, Osita. Afam went into a tantrum and refused to go.

' "I want my toys — the toys my brother Osita sent me from England. I want my toys."

'Charles, to Maria's dismay, lost his temper, and

dragged the howling boy out of the sitting room. Maria found herself apologising for Charles' behaviour to her neighbours who had come to welcome her.

' "We should be apologising to you, your welcome should not be spoilt by Afam's tantrums! You and your husband are going to find raising Afam a really big job. His character is almost formed and he has been encouraged to have his way with his grand-parents ... " Mrs Cooker, Maria's neighbour and old friend, began. She could not continue however as Afam's howls filled the apartment. Maria could hear stones being thrown and glasses smashing. She looked at Mrs Cooker in fear.

'And her friend nodded mutely as if to say, this is what it has been these past months.

'Maria got up and was about to go into the inner room to help Charles hush the boy when Dr Cooker, who was also there, urged her firmly into a chair. "Sit there, Maria, this is not your funeral, your husband's name is Ubakanma, the crowd is better. Well he's got one son too many for his crowd, let him deal with him. And you be careful with that boy, his mother's tongue is sharper than you realise."

' "Is the mother here?" Maria asked, aghast.

'Mrs Cooker looked at Maria with that sympathy which only women can feel for each other. She shook her head. "Thank goodness, she left just two weeks ago. But what a fight she put up when Charles told her to go back because you were returning. It was then we knew what was happening. We were wondering who she was. I thought she was a new maid, but she soon left us in no doubt at all. It was devastating for Charles. To go to all this trouble simply because he wanted more children."

' "Well, people are much more valuable than money," Dr Cooker put in pompously to defend the childishness of his sex.

'The two ladies looked at each other and agreed that yes, people are more valuable than money, but what they did not ask was what type of people. Maria and Charles were soon to find out that what they had had previously was certainly more valuable than certain kinds of people.

8 Raising Afam

'Auntie Bintu, there is nothing as irksome as raising another woman's child all alone if that woman is a person like Obioma, Afam's mother. Afam completely refused to be tamed. Maria could not be too strict with him because people would have said that she never wanted him in the first place. She could not report most of mischievousness to Charles for fear of being accused of poisoning Charles' mind against his son. So she had to put up with the boy's tantrums.'

'But did they not send the boy to school?'

'Well, they did, Auntie Bintu. Maria would dress the boy smartly — by then her anger had cooled over Charles — for she took pride in taking the boy to the very private primary school that Osita had attended. But as soon as Afam was nine and able to walk to school by himself, he chose a different kind of amusement. He would pretend to be going to school but would actually go to the lagoon to pick crabs. And then when teachers complained to his father, Afam would resort to throwing things and hurling abuse at them. This went on so much that he became an embarrassment to the school. After all parents paid all those exorbitant fees so that their children could be exposed to other well behaved ones from respectable families. So they had to ask Charles and Maria to remove him from their school.

'You can imagine Charles' disappointment at this. They shunted him from school to school with no success, and of course the relationship between him and his father became worse.

'Soon he became so big and strong that Maria could no longer smack him or tell him off. She then tried the art of gentle persuasion, assuring him that she loved him and that he was very much wanted in the family. One day she went through this session with him while Afam sat through it quietly, pretending to be interested in all that Maria was saying. So it was a shock to Maria one day when she returned from work, early in the afternoon, to hear the sounds of young voices cursing, stamping and spitting at something. At first she did not know what it was.

'That afternoon was very hot and Maria had had a bad morning at the hospital with patients and the young nurses under her. She was looking forward to a cool bath and a long rest, before she got ready to prepare for the evening meal. She had driven in quietly and gone into the house through the back door. As she passed the side of the house, she saw several young heads, laughing and apparently enjoying themselves. She wondered who was there. Afam should have been at the special Remedial Centre where they had started sending him. So Maria thought at first that burglars might have broken in. Charles would not be in until a couple of hours later, she knew.

'Consequently she noiselessly tiptoed into the kitchen. You see their apartment was built in such a way that you could enter the living room through the kitchen. Those places were built in what we call open-plan here. Well, she armed herself with a brick ready to throw and make a run for it, but when she looked in she saw that Afam was there. But what were the children doing? They were about the six roughest boys you could pick up from that part of Ikoyi.'

'But, Amina, is Ikoyi not still the most expensive part of Lagos?'

'It is, Auntie Bintu. It is not only the most expensive but the most select and only God knows where Afam had picked his crowd from.'

'Maybe from the Remedial Centre,' I prompted.

Amina looked at me hard and I could see what she was thinking. She came to her conclusion within a few seconds and shrugged her shoulders. 'Maybe from the Remedial Centre, but, Auntie Bintu, what did one expect Charles and Maria to do? They sent him to a good fee-paying school where he could meet with the best children in Lagos, but he was expelled and they could not just keep him at home could they?'

'I know, Amina, I'm not blaming Charles and Maria. What I'm saying is that sometimes when young people are sent to such places they come in contact with worse people. It's like when you send a young offender to a big prison, he comes in contact with the hardened law-breakers, and he may come out worse and ready to commit even more horrible crimes. But don't let me make you lose the thread of your story, please go on.'

'Yes, Auntie Bintu. When Maria tiptoed through the kitchen she saw that the cans of beer Charles kept in the fridge were scattered all over the room. She saw from the way the boys were behaving that they were drunk, but what amazed her was the way they were standing. They had formed a circle and were cursing something in the middle of the circle. Some were spitting at it, others were shouting things like, "May you roast in fire, for ever and ever. May you never come home ... " and Afam was urging them on to put the greatest verbal damnation they could think of on the object. But when the boys started to say things like, "May you never come home from England, and may you never qualify as a doctor so that our friend here will inherit all Ubakanma's wealth ... " Afam burst out laughing. The laughter was hysterical, ringing eerily from one corner of the apartment to another. It was not the laughter of an innocent thirteen-year-old, but the laughter of a wild animal.

'Maria then forgot her fear and rushed into the room with, "What in the name of God are you up to now Afam?" The boys, not expecting her there, were taken aback. A few made for the door, but one or two hurled the cans they were holding at the intruder. Afam picked up the object they had been cursing and then Maria saw that it was Osita's latest picture, the picture she had only just recently had framed, showing him in the whites of his trade with a stethoscope showing in his pocket. Osita had written to her about the picture saying, "Mother a future doctor DV," and they had all laughed. Afam, too, had laughed when it arrived, and how proud Charles had been at the distinguished figure his son Osita was cutting. "We must frame it," he had declared.

' "Oh Charles, but it's only a black and white photo, why can't you wait until he sends one in his academic robes?"

' "Oh no, Maria, we must frame it, so that our young

man here can always be reminded of the fact that if he worked hard he too could become anything he wanted."

'The nasty smile on Afam's face had disappeared immediately and turned into a scowl and he had murmured, "Doctors are not necessarily rich people. I saw a doctor the other day who was a beggar!"

' "Shut up!" Charles had thundered.

' "Oh Charles, he is right. Not all doctors are rich, but Afam you must pray that your brother will be one of the successful ones." Then Maria had left the room.

' "Listen Afam, who told you that doctors are not necessarily the richest people?" Maria heard Charles ask as she was leaving the room.

'Afam had assumed an air of mysterious importance and said airily, "Hmm one picks up things from here and there, Father."

' "Who told you?" Charles' voice was raised. His nerves had been jarred by the constant worries over this boy, his mother and his job. So he, too, was becoming more and more impatient. Maybe he was realising his mistakes — that good and socially strong women almost invariably produced children who worked hard and produced socially approved results.

' "Who told you?" he thundered again.

' "All right, all right, sometimes my friends, sometimes my mother, so what have I done wrong, enh? I can't even take part in any conversation any more . . . "

'But Charles did not allow him to end his sentence. Charles, that quietly-spoken man with an easy manner, Charles, that man who was always smiling . . . Do you know, Auntie Bintu, I still cannot imagine Charles hitting anyone? But they said that that night, he beat Afam so much that the boy ran away to report his father at the police station.'

'Oh my God, so Nigerian children have started doing that as well. It is happening in Europe.'

'It is not common here, though. You find it occasionally among the sons of the rich, you know the children who have been given everything. You know that Maria took Afam to the UK twice to see his brother, and sometimes Osita would come home for a week. So Afam was not an ignoramus. He "knew his rights" as they say he was always quoting to his parents.'

'So, Amina, what did the police do?'

'They sent him back home after caning him. You know our policemen . . . well most of them are fathers themselves, and would not like to encourage the wilful young, and when that young person is the son of a second unpopular wife of the Permanent Secretary to the Ministry of Labour, you as a policeman would not like to take chances.

'Afam swallowed his pride and seemed superficially to have settled down, knowing that there was no escape; he had to toe the line. I think that was where he had got the idea of cursing his brother's picture. He could not reach him physically but he could reach his picture.

'Maria snatched the picture, now shattered, and clutched it to her chest and started to howl. She cried from shock and anger. She cried at what Allah had done to Charles and herself. She cried because of the unfairness of the whole thing. She was still in that state of shock and unhappiness when Charles came into the house a few hours later.

'Maria was sitting dejected on the floor, clutching

Osita's photo to her chest and blood was trickling from her forehead where the boys in fear had thrown the cans of beer at her. Charles' shock was beyond words.

'He picked up the wife Allah had given him in the first place, the wife whose fate had been originally knotted up with his before he had allowed himself to be pushed into a situation he knew he did not really want, and they both cried.

'They said that the sun was partially down in the west when they started to cry, but they clung to each other and cried after the sun had completely disappeared. At length their evening maid came; and she was a nice girl who had the presence of mind to call their friends the Cookers. They all decided that the best thing would be to send Afam back home to Ibusa to be with his mother.'

'Well a bad son always belongs to the mother, does he not? And a good one to the father?' I shook my head. 'It still has not changed, has it?'

'No, Auntie Bintu,' Amina replied, agreeing with me.

9 Afam's return to Ibusa

'You know what they say, Auntie Bintu; when troubles come to anyone they do not come singly but in droves,' Amina began, eyeing me mysteriously.

'That is very true,' I agreed, nodding.

'A person's behaviour is like smoke, it is impossibe to hide. Maria had tried very much to hide Afam's mischievousness from people but word had seeped through to most of their friends in Lagos of how bad and uncontrollable the boy was. So, though many people knew that at that time Charles could not get away from his place of work, yet none agreed to take Afam home for him. Those of their friends who wished to go home kept the knowledge from Charles and Maria. Meanwhile Afam, knowing what his fate would be in Ibusa, started to use another tactic. He became cool and began to plead with them.

' "I will do anything you ask me to do. I am sorry about what happened, truly I am. Please don't send me back to Ibusa. I am happy here, Father. Please, Mummy, say something."

'But his father Charles, and who could blame him, was determined to send him back to his grandparents. Shame kills faster than disease and Charles was a very quiet person who minded his own business; you know he was very English in some ways. But this son of his, Afam, had allowed people to know most of their

secrets. Charles, like most quiet men, did not like that
at all. He and Maria were reduced to the state of
having to explain all their behaviour to this teacher,
that neighbour and that policeman. It was not an
enviable position for the Permanent Secretary to the
Ministry of Labour to be in.

'As no one would take Afam, his father decided to
do it himself. He packed everything ready for the boy
to go home to Ibusa, but on the night before, Afam
disappeared.'

'Oh my God, Amina, for a boy to disappear in a place
like Lagos! What a worrying position to put his
parents in,' I cried reminding myself of how long the
list of missing people is in a metropolis like Lagos.

'I know, Auntie Bintu. That was when the whole
of the city, as well most of the country, came to know
about it. People searched everywhere. Charles had to
give dash to this policeman and more to that one. The
papers carried Maria's story. You could guess the
insinuations: she could no longer have a child of her
own, so she had probably put a curse on Afam; she
was probably telling lies about the cursing and
spitting on her son's photograph. Some women
journalists wanted to know why Maria should be that
upset about a little boy's pranks.

'Maria threatened to leave Charles many many
times, but each time she packed the things she
remembered the days they had had together. Those
happy days that now seemed to belong to another
world. She also noticed that her husband Charles was
not able to cope alone. He became withdrawn and his
head started to go bald. Some say that sometimes he
would not eat for days. They both stopped worrying
about Afam but instead looked closely at each other.

Had Charles, knowing himself to be a monogamous person, been right in allowing his ageing parents to intrude into their idyllic life to the point of almost ruining it?

' "They did not mean us any harm," Charles maintained. "They wanted Osita to have a brother, and you would have gained a son, too."

' "Yes, I would have gained not only a son but Obioma and her little daughter as well. As I said, I am getting tired of people phoning to ask me what the latest news is about Afam. And the more they do that the more I blame myself for revealing what he did on Osita's photo."

' "If Afam had been your real son and not Obioma's would you not have done the same? You would have. So let's just pray that he turns up and is not in any danger."

'The very evening after this conversation, Charles decided to take some exercise and he went for a walk around Ikoyi Crescent where they lived. To his surprise he saw someone who looked like Obioma, Afam's mother, coming out of a bus. On getting closer Charles could not mistake the slight woman with her swaying walk. Afam's mother had that easy walk peculiar to Ibusa women with a little wealth. Though she was not born into this wealth she had acquired it by the maintenance Charles was sending her. But what was she doing here in Lagos? Charles wondered.

' "Obioma," Charles called gently. She turned, looking confused.

'Charles opened and closed his mouth like a fish gasping for air. A child could have knocked Charles off the road as he stood there gaping at this woman who his parents had thrust at him. Once he had been sorry for the girl and had found her obedience touching. She had flattered his ego as a man, because of her dependency. But that was all Obioma could give him. Though Charles was now in the Ministry of Labour he still had his eyes on the Foreign Service. And he could not dream of presenting someone like Obioma as his wife even though she would have been wife number two. Many of his friends had many wives, but this was something he did not want to indulge in, not whilst he was still working. He would think about it in retirement, if Maria did not produce another child. He had left it like that until his mother started to urge him to come home and look at this land they were negotiating for him. He could remember how very nervous he had been the first night with Obioma. His father had said that they were thinking of getting another young girl to help Maria with housework, and that this second woman could be his wife number two if he wanted. He had not paid any particular attention to what his father was saying until he felt Obioma in his bed at the dead of the night.

'He jumped up and protested to his parents. The girl began to cry and his mother told him that he was condemning an innocent girl to a life of shame if he did not go to bed with her. She said that Obioma would never be able to marry anyone else because people would always refer to her as Charles Ubakanma's cast off. No one would believe that Charles had not had anything to do with her. For they would ask, how can Charles Ubakanma not fancy a girl so young and so beautiful that her body could wake the dead? There must be something wrong with Charles himself, and not with Maria, could have been the rumour.

' "Is there something wrong with you, son? Are you impotent and are you not man enough to admit it? Will you allow people to blame it on your wife Maria?"

' "Of course I am all right," Charles replied irritably.

' "Then why don't you prove it to your people? After all we have paid for her and she doesn't have to come and stay with you over there. She is very young and will be there waiting for you."

'The argument had gone on almost till morning when his cousin, Uchechuwu, who was of the same age as him, suggested that, as the argument was going to go on all night, they should drink and celebrate the arrival of the new bride Obioma. Somehow the rest of the night was blurred. He remembered the superior feeling he felt when he was making love to Obioma, who was then little more than a child. His feeling of guilt had to be deadened and he heard himself promising to look after her. When a few months later word came to him that Obioma was pregnant, he was afraid of what Maria would do and at the same time happy that everything had turned out as his mother had said. Now he knew that the fault of their infertility was not his but Maria's.

'He was at home to witness Afam's naming ceremony. "Afamefuna — may my name not be lost or forgotten," his parents had called the new baby. Charles could guess from the name given to the child how anxious his parents had been on his account. He was an only son, and is parents did not want their grandson Osita to be an only son as well. "Others will start claiming our land before our very eyes and say after all we can produce only one son in each generation," his father had said.

' "What are you doing in Lagos and whose baby are you carrying, Obioma," Charles asked brutally as they stood in the middle of the sidewalk at Ikoyi Crescent.

' "I arrived in Lagos two days ago, and was just going to your place to tell you and your wife Maria that Afam is now in Ibusa, but that I cannot look after him. I want to marry someone else, and he will not let Afam live with us."

'Charles stood there looking at this woman, and at the thick green bushes that edged the Crescent. He had no right to call her Judas. She was very young, and it had been unfair to make a woman he did not love the mother of his son and daughter.

' "Who is looking after the baby, Obioma?" he asked on finding his voice.

' "My mother is."

' "You don't need to come and tell me at home. I will tell Maria. And thank you for relieving us of our suspense. I will go home in a few weeks and arrange the proper places for the children."

' "Your parents will gladly have them, but Afam is very difficult, even with me, to say nothing of the old people. I don't know why he is so rebellious and unhappy."

' "I don't know either," Charles said as he retraced his steps to his home in Ikoyi. The twilight suddenly disappeared and it was dark before he reached his home. He told Maria what he had just seen, and she asked him if he was sure he had not been dreaming.

'A telephone call from Asaba the following day told both Maria and Charles that Charles had not been dreaming. Afam was at home. But what a terror he had become!

10 Charles in Ibusa

'Charles Ubakanma had been dozing most of the journey home but woke up as the new smell of Ibusa surroundings hit his nostrils. The beauty of that part of our country had never ceased to surprise him, its thick forests, red footpaths and the tarred road winding in and out of the green forest like a thick black snake.

'It was a mild evening when Charles arrived in Ibusa in response to the appeal of his fast ageing parents. They had been ageing gradually before, like every other old couple, but since Obioma had thrust Afam on to them, the ageing process had become so much faster. Today the father would say he had foot-ache, tomorrow the mother would say that her arm ached, but they were all psychological complaints!

'But, Amina, should Charles and his parents not have taken care of Afam instead of expecting Obioma to do it? They dragged her from her father's house to marry their son Charles. And Charles gave her Afam, so why should she carry the can?'

'Auntie Bintu, Charles did not want Afam to stay with his mother, especially now that she was married to another family. But Afam had left Lagos secretly and instead of going to his grandparents went to his mother. So Charles thought that he chose his mother because he was happier with her.'

'But Afam did not know that his mother was then busy negotiating another marriage for herself.'

'But Auntie Bintu, can you blame Obioma? When a woman is very young and in her teens, it is all right to be told that her husband is the Permanent Secretary to this or that ministry. But as the years roll by, and she finds she is expected to see her husband only once or twice a year, the glamour of being the wife of a big man wears off. Anyone could see that Maria was not a chicken-livered woman who would take to her heels and run at the mere rumour of a storm.'

'That is very true, Amina. And Charles their husband did not want Maria to go either. The irony of it all was that most of those people who arranged and accepted Obioma's bride-price simply gaped and said very little.'

'What could they say? They had led a girl to a rich family; and a rich family meant security to them. They also thought that because Obioma was much younger than Maria, and because she still had many children in her whilst Maria was almost barren, Charles would allow her to come and live with them in Lagos. They were wrong. Some men like Charles behave almost like Europeans because of their long exposure to that culture.'

'Look Amina, some white men do the same, you know. They have mistresses, and play a double game with their wives. The only faithful Englishmen I've known are the very old ones. When they become old, they are frightened in case their wives should leave them to live alone as this usually hastens their death. In middle-age, however, they take this secretary on a trip here and another on a trip there. Men are all the same, but their women are now bolder, standing up to their men.'

'Auntie Bintu, that kind of boldness will take a long time to happen here! Anyway, when Charles got home he saw with his own eyes what he had been dreading. Obioma was settled in a new home, her little daughter was left with Charles' mother, as was Afam, who had by now grown almost as tall as Charles, but stronger. There was little Charles could do except accept the refund of Obioma's bride-price. He pleaded with the Irish Reverend Fathers and they accepted Afam at a school called Saint Thomas's in Ibusa. He could not saddle Maria with another child, so he left the little girl Nneka with his own mother, Madam Ubakanma.

'But now Big Mama Ubaka began to complain. She was too old and could not look after Nneka. She said Maria should take care of the child because in Lagos Nneka would be exposed to a richer life than they could give her in Ibusa. You must not forget, Auntie Bintu that Big Mama Ubaka was not originally from Ibusa, otherwise she would have taken pride in looking after Nneka, a job which any grandmother born in Ibusa would have not only delighted in doing but would have taken pride in. Nonetheless, Charles refused. And for the first time in their lives there was a big confrontation between son and parents, so bitter that people still talk about it.

' "You ruined my life," Charles cried. "My peace of mind and my happiness are gone because you wished me to live up to my family name, Ubakanma. Do people with no children get thrown to the vultures? Don't they all get buried? Do they say that childless people will not go to heaven or hell or wherever dead people go? We all get buried under six foot of earth, whether we have fifty children or are child free. What matters to me is a happy and peaceful private life. Now everybody knows my story; the story of Maria's barrenness is repeated from mouth to mouth, so much so that people now tend to forget that she had Osita — Osita who is doing so well and will soon qualify as a doctor. You all forced me to have this devil of a boy you call Afam — may my name not be lost. If his sister comes to live with us, I will not only lose my name but will definitely lose my sanity. You look after her, Mother. Did you not name her Nneka — mother is the greatest? Then look after her, I will send you all the money you need from Lagos, but she stays here and this is final."

' "No, that is not final," Big Papa Ubakanma, who had been listening to his son with mounting anger, cried. "That is not the final word. As long as I am alive, I have the final say in this house. Charles, the son of Ubakanma, you are selfish. That England you went to and those white people you are aping have made you selfish. You want your happiness and peace of mind! But how, my son, can somebody have happiness and peace of mind if all those who love that person are in mental turmoil? Tell me how. When you have that happiness are you and your wife Maria going to live on an island all by yourself and enjoy that happiness? Do you know how many deaths your mother and myself die when you let us know you are travelling from one town to the other? When as a child you had a slight cold or a mild attack of malaria, we virtually stopped living. So when you married Maria, we thought that you two would make it up for all of us. If you had had another brother or sister, we would not have demanded so much of you, but you are the only one we have, and we prayed that your life with Maria would not be like ours. But then Maria had only Osita. Nobody blames her, it was not her fault; it was only that the position as it was then was making everybody in this family jumpy. I could not go to any elders' meeting and talk with conviction because I kept worrying that the only person I had to give me immortality was Osita. And if anything (God forbid) should happen to that boy, the Ubakanma's line is dead, dead forever. Already there are vultures hovering over the land of our fathers. So we simply have to make alternative arrangements. Don't they do it in Europe as well? Families adopting children or bringing in children born out of wedlock?"

' "Afam was not born out of wedlock," Big Mama Ubakanma put in. "He is Charles' son, our grandson, conceived in this house!"

' "I know, Anasi, I am just saying. You know, Charles, what they say is that there is immortality. Maybe so, but to me the immortality I understand is my offspring. If there is no direct line from a person, then that person has no immortality, that's what makes life interesting. Who would live through a life full of happiness and peace all the time? Everybody would either start killing themselves out of boredom or the madhouse would be full of insane people."

'Charles looked coolly at his parents. He had never been so angry with them before, and now was simply fed up with living their lives for them. His father may have been right, but that was his world. He did not subscribe wholly to it. So he asked a question which he regretted to his dying day.

' "If you know all this, Father, why did you not marry another woman?"

'For a moment, Mama Ubakanma looked as if she was going to faint or drop down dead. And to add to Charles' astonishment, his father began to cry. Madam Ubakanma collected herself quickly, stepped up to her son Charles, and slapped him on both cheeks, a thing she had never done, even when Charles was a little boy. "What kind of a stupid, selfish man have I reared as a son?" she wailed.

'Obi Ubakanma stepped up to his son and said, "All right, all right, I'll tell you. After you, I could not father any more children because of an accident I had in my work-place."

'They said that tears filled Charles' eyes and he dashed out of their house, called his driver and ordered him to drive back to Lagos.

'And as for Afam, who had caused all this unhappiness, he left the school his father had put him in and came back to the village as soon as he knew that his father had left for Lagos. He stayed in that school, for which his father had used his position as a Permanent Secretary to the Ministry of Labour, for only four weeks. The Catholic Reverend Fathers did their best to keep him there, but Afam would not stay. They worked so hard and prayed so fervently for that boy Afam that when he left they all felt they had earned the dash Charles Ubakanma gave them in the form of goats, turkeys and plenty of eggs.

11 Osita's graduation ceremony

'They say that when Maria and Charles arrived in London for the graduation of their son Osita, the sun was shining. It was not raining and it was not cold and all the parks, the front and back gardens of the houses in London were full of sweet smelling roses.'

'What month was it, Amina? Did you find that out?'

'They said that the couple arrived at the end of May or first week in June, something like that, I am not absolutely sure,' Amina replied with a shrug, wondering no doubt why I should interrupt her narration for such a minor incident like the weather. Little did she know that those of us living in London are obsessed with the weather. We talk about it almost every day, we plan around it, and worry about it. And it is always the safest subject of conversation. But to Amina, the sun always shone, and there was very little change from one season to another. The slight change was the heavy rains, but that did not stop the sun from shining.

'It was easy for Charles and Maria to feel as if this visit to London, the town in which they met as students those long years ago, was their second honeymoon,' Amina continued. 'Mind you, Auntie Bintu, Maria had been coming to see her son whilst he was at Medical School, but Charles had never followed her. But this time he came with her, not just to see their son's graduation but as a break from the tension in his family. Afam did not improve, he became worse; Madam Ubakanma became ill and died only a few months afterwards.'

'Oh, Amina, so Mama Badagry is dead. I am sorry to hear it. And of course Charles and Maria would be riddled with guilt.'

'You've got it Auntie Bintu. You know when people die in your family, you who are still alive go through a period of self-condemnation, torturing yourself that maybe there was something, just something you could have done to save the dead person from going. And when the dead relative was your mother, and a mother you loved as dearly as Charles loved his mother, and then towards the end you had had a slight misunderstanding, well the guilt was even heavier. Charles completely withdrew into himself saying that it was the argument he had had with his mother that killed her. He would not be comforted for a very long time.'

'So what happened to Obi Ubakanma?'

'I think they got him a new wife or something like that.'

'Surely not a sixteen-year-old, Amina?'

'No, no, Obi Ubakanma was too sensible for such a thing. He knew how incapacitated he had been rendered by his accident, so all he wanted was a housekeeper. But this woman, who had passed her middle years, wanted a house to live in. So Charles and Maria encouraged the marriage; that way the woman would stay longer, hopefully.'

I began to laugh. Amina's eyes bored inside me trying to find out what it was that I found so amusing.

'You know what I call that type of marriage? The

practical marriage of convenience. Obi Ubakanma wanted a housekeeper and the new woman wanted a home. So by marrying her, he would not have to pay her, and she would not like to go away easily.'

'Ah, but Auntie Bintu, the Obi must have paid her people for her bride-price.'

'Yes, he would have returned his bride-price of about fifty naira to her former husband's people. And for that fifty naira, the Obi would have secured her services for the rest of her life. I keep arguing that bride-prices are not just gift tokens but a kind of price of woman-selling.'

'Oh well, Auntie Bintu, we in our part of the country don't do it, well not to the extent practised by the Ibos. But the Obi would give this new woman his protection and his name. The Ubakanma's family had got a good name despite Afam and Maria's barrenness. Oh stop laughing, Auntie Bintu, Maria's barrenness after all started all the trouble. If she had produced as many children as the family thought she would, the old people would not have forced Obioma on Charles. So although it was not her fault, yet it was a slur on the family. But now that Osita was graduating at a Hall in London, the parents felt as if they had ten children instead of just Osita. They sat there in their seats and watched their son proceed with the other graduates past the Chancellor of his University. Oh it was beautiful to see the pride on their faces. What they did not know was that the young woman sitting right next to them and smiling at them all through the ceremony was Ruth, Osita's sweetheart whom he had promised to marry as soon as they got home to Nigeria.

'The ceremony was soon over, and Charles invited

his son and a few friends to a posh hotel in Park Lane for a celebration dinner. It was when Charles was embracing his son and saying things like, "Congratulations, my son, my very hearty congratulations," that Osita held his father at arms' length and said proudly, "Mother, Father, this is Ruth, a friend of mine, em, more than a friend, a very special friend who's agreed to be your daughter, Mother."

'Ruth said that they embraced her in such a way that for a time she was frightened of being crushed. Maria was so happy. Ruth is a beautiful girl, not just physical beauty, but her behaviour is beyond reproach. What strikes me about her is that she is a highly academic person who does not indulge in things like hair perming or straightening. She only trims her hair and the neatness this gives her face is almost virginal. She is small, not as fair as Osita, and her large eyes are shaped liked almonds, and have the colour of fresh water. She seldom speaks but smiles a great deal, and, as if an added grace, she is from Ibusa. That would have delighted big Mama Ubakanma, had she lived to see this day.

'It was agreed that Ruth should come and join Osita at the end of her course to give Osita time to finish his Youth Call. As for Charles and Maria, they had never spent such a relaxing and problem-free time since their student days. They visited places they used to know, checked up their former landladies who were now getting on and were all so pleased to see them and happy to be remembered. They travelled outside London, went visiting, and Maria even had a short stay on a health farm. So it was a nice healthy, happy and relaxed couple that boarded the Nigeria Airways plane back to Lagos, a month after they had left.

'People, their friends, noticed the change in Charles and Maria. She had been beginning to let herself go with worries and a sense of insecurity, but after the visit she became confident in Charles and began to take care of her looks. Charles went back to work like a completely new man. You see, Auntie Bintu, apart from the rest and the cool English summer, Osita gave them that inner confidence that comes from knowing that one's child has succeeded. He might have been wrong with Afam, but he was right with Osita. So, when Charles was with his friends it was all the time, "My son the doctor said this, my son the doctor said that and he did the other thing ... "

'Yes, Amina, does it not come to what I always say, that a bad child belongs to the mother and a good one to the father? I wonder if Charles at that stage remembered Maria's sacrifice and determination to invest all her income on their son?'

'I don't even think that people talked about that at all. Osita was Charles' successful son. After all, was Charles not a Permanent Secretary and Maria only a nurse? Who would believe her story? But their son Osita knew, and the good man told his sweetheart Ruth. They kept the knowledge to themselves and allowed Charles to bask in the joys of success. Well, after all, was he not the biological father?'

'You're right, Amina. It was a good thing Osita did not fail his mother Maria, that would have killed her. And with Ruth and their soon-to-happen marriage I can see her saying to herself, "Now I have so many things to look forward to." And she would be right to think so.'

12 Afam

'In the olden days, when men took the Obi title, they were stopped from being Christians, because the white people who brought Christianity to those parts said that taking such titles was barbaric and therefore evil. But then many of our people started going to the white men's countries and found to their surprise that one could be a Lord or an Earl or a Lady and still be a Christian. So many people became determined to keep their Christianity and their titles. Some Catholic priests protested in places like Ibusa, but had to stop their protestations when suddenly they found themselves preaching their gospels to bare walls. People, and in particular rich men, stopped coming to worship and some even went as far as to form their own churches. After all Christianity did not just belong to one race.'

'It should not be like that. Just like our Muslim religion, it has no racial boundaries,' I agreed.

'Yes, Auntie Bintu, that is a common knowledge but you must remember that not so long ago those who called themselves Christians always behaved as if they were a cut above the rest of us.'

'I know what you mean, Amina; our independence changed all that. We were ruled by the people who brought Christianity. Sometimes I doubt the reason for their bringing it to us, because though England is a Christian country, yet one can't really call them church-going people.'

'Auntie Bintu, what do they do on Sundays then when they are not in church? How can people be Christians when they don't go to their places of worship? It's like saying you can be a good Muslim but never visit your local mosque.'

'I know it sounds odd Amina, but it is true. They love animals because animals cannot speak for themselves and on the whole they can be compassionate and caring, especially on the individual level. Their government always puts their country first and that is not very Christian. But the Queen goes to church, and as for the ordinary people, my neighbours for instance, they wash their cars and do their gardens on Sundays.'

'But they told us that if Christians do not go to church they will be burned in hell fire,' Amina spat. 'How hypocritical can one be?'

'I know. They are closing many of the churches or turning them into community meeting places. And yet they once insisted on such ridiculous laws like stopping a Nigerian titled man from worshipping his creator the way he wanted.'

'Well thanks be to Allah, all that has changed now. When Madam Ubakanma died, they buried her with both Christian and the native prayers. And her people from Badagry, who worshipped Ogun, came and said their own prayers and sacrificed with dogs.'

'*Wallai*, that lady went down with so many prayers!'

'Yes, Auntie Bintu, she really did and her husband mourned her for the usual twenty-one days. After the period of mourning, he went to church for thanksgiving and then this lady came to offer her condolences.

'Obi Ubakanma saw her, and liked her gentle manner. She was a retiring woman who had lost her husband and whose children were scattered all over the world and so busy that they did not think much about home — to say nothing of their mother. So this lady, Madam Ngbeke, threw her lot into the church. There she made friends and became a very important although quiet member of Women's Prayer Meeting.

'Obi Ubakanma could not believe his luck when Madam Ngbeke offered to come and clean for him every market day. Soon, a kind of mutual understanding developed to which Maria and Charles gave all their blessing at the right time. The Obi found himself getting married within a few months of his wife's death. What the Ubakanma's family did not know was that, though Madam Ngbeke came to church regularly looking clean and happy, she was a poor woman who in her late fifties still had to go into the bush to fetch firewood to sell in order to make a living. Now she was going to move into a big house and marry a man who was on pension and had a son like Charles.

'A friend of Madam Ngbeke's, you know how such friends take it upon themselves to warn one, said to her one day, "You know the Ubakas have a very troublesome son called Afam. This boy is so bold that he fought the Permanent Secretary's wife and his mother is that showy woman called Obioma."

' "Well, my friend," Madam Ngbeke said, "I believe in the power of prayers. If I do not snatch this opportunity that God is giving me to be happy, I will never have one like it again."

' "The man needs a housekeeper, and if he dies, they may throw you out."

' "Well, my friend, a happy housekeeper is better than a wood carrier and with a person like Charles as a stepson, I will not be thrown out if the Obi dies. You never know, if I look after him well, he may still live for many years. And how do we know that I am going to outlive him? Death is a debt we all must pay."

' "Well, Ngbeke, don't say I did not warn you."

' "Thank you, my friend, and for that warning I will make sure that I buy all the wood I need from you, when I become the Obi's wife, because I will be too busy looking after the house to go out for firewood. I am sure the Obi will not allow his wife to carry firewood."

'So the friend went away hurt, but Madam Ngbeke was not frightened of Afam. In fact she let the boy do exactly what he wanted. All Madam Ngbeke wanted was a roof over her head and she was not going to allow any stupid squabble over a spoilt child to ruin it for her. If the Obi asked, "But what is Afam doing these days?" she would reply and say, "Obi, the son of Ubakanma, the husband of Ngbeke, Afam is busy living his life like all young men. He goes to the farm to help the labourers and goes to dance with his friends in the evening. One thing you must be sure of, Obi, he always has his meals on time." The Obi was getting old and tired and did not want any trouble with Afam as well.

'It was Charles who was not only worried but took steps to make the boy do something with his life. As soon as Afam knew that his father was visiting Ibusa, he would disappear from his grandfather's and go and terrorise his mother — in her new home. Charles knew this and determined to catch the boy at his game.

'One day, after his visit to London, Charles suddenly arrived in Ibusa. Having parked his car a long way away, he sneaked into their compound, where he saw Afam swallowing pounded yam laced with thick *egusi* soup that Madam Ngbeke had cooked.

' "Hello father," Afam gulped.

' "I understand you're now helping our workers on the farm. Should you not be there on the farm now?" Charles asked, ignorning Afam's surprised greeting.

' "Well, I did not go there today."

' "Why not, are you ill?"

' "I will go tomorrow, Father."

' "You will go tomorrow. So who is looking after the labourers today? My father pays them to work and pays you to supervise. He pays them knowing that you'll be there to help and to see that they work for their money, and here you are shamelessly swallowing pounded yams made from yams you never worked for."

'Afam had by then been spoilt by his Ibusa upbringing, specially as he knew that the old Obi could do little about him. So he was not afraid to reply sarcastically to anyone. He was not even afraid of his father Charles. To him Charles was just another adult to be insulted.'

'I don't know, Amina, maybe Afam loved his father dearly, but he in turn had rejected him and his mother because he was not a success.'

'Oh, Auntie Bintu, but Maria and Charles did all they could for him and he refused their helping hands.

How can the world go round blaming his father?'

'Amina, I am not blaming anyone. I am just saying, if Charles had married a third wife, Afam probably would not have seen his father just as Maria's husband but as a father for all of them. Maybe that would have helped.'

Amina shook her head. 'A bad person is a bad person. Most children take after their mothers you know, Auntie Bintu. If one's mother is strong and determined to make the best of herself, her children usually come out right because they copy what they see.'

'You have a point there, but it does not always follow. I know that people in China held this view at one time, so much so that they once recommended that only female graduates should have the right to bring children into the world.'

'Anyway, Auntie Bintu, Afam was rude to his father. He got up, kicked the food and said, "I work for the yams as well." He was ready to run if his father should lose his temper. But Charles knew better. He just said coolly, "Look, Afam, I have recently been to see your brother in the UK. He is now qualified as a doctor. You'll have no right to blame anyone in the future but yourself. We sent you to the same school but you refused to work hard. Don't go round in future saying that Osita did not help you, when you refused to help yourself."

' "Oh, for God's sake. I am fed up with hearing of Osita's achievements. Doctors now don't get much money anyway. I will be rich. It's your son Osita who will come and beg money from me, not me from him," he spat and stalked away.

'The adults present simply looked at each other.

Each one was asking himself or herself the question most disappointed parents have for generations asked themselves. "Where have we gone wrong? What have we done to deserve this from our child?"

13 Get rich quick

'Auntie Bintu, we should not blame Afam for thinking that it was easy to get rich quickly without having to work hard. He had apparently seen men and women who had never gone to school riding around in big cars and living well. So when Charles warned him about his future, he could afford to boast and say "You do not have to be a doctor or even be educated to be rich."

'Yes, it is the word "rich" that you keep hearing, not education. If you are highly educated in this place and have no obvious money to back it up, you are not respected.'

Amina started one of her spontaneous laughs when I said this. She took the last bottle of wine on our table and poured the rest of it into her glass. I thought to myself, well a good Muslim is not supposed to drink at all. But I did not say anything to her out loud. I only asked, 'What is so funny now?'

Amina drank the wine and said, 'You know why I'm laughing Auntie Bintu. When some of you people first return from the UK, you always seem to have this noble idea of not wanting to pollute the atmosphere and not wanting to ride in any cars, so you start going about on foot until you realise that people stop respecting you. Then you go back and start living like everybody else, with cars and all the modern conveniences.

'Then the fault is not with those of us who want to live the simple life, but with the government. The money spent in giving out car loans could be used in providing workable public transport for all. The government would only spend a fraction of the loans they give now, and there would be fewer cars on the road and fewer accidents. But now what do you have? Every market woman uses a car to take her modest wares to her local market. So young boys like Afam regard huge cars as evidence of success rather than a string of exam successes.'

'There are some genuine business people though, Auntie Bintu.'

'Oh yes, who's doubting that. But when everybody becomes a business man or woman and all wish to be equally successful, then you have problems. So what business did Afam get involved with, Amina?'

'Em,' Amina started with obvious hesitancy. My mind went back to her former boyfriend who got involved in drug trafficking. I kept quiet, respecting her unwillingness to talk about some of our 'businesses'.

'First, as I hinted before, he started to catch fish in the Oboshi stream. He and his friends would go there, catch the fish, however young, and try to make their fortunes by asking high prices for them. Then people refused to buy and the fish usually went bad in a couple of hours. They would then be forced to sell them cheaply or give them away.'

'They should have bought a fridge.'

'A fridge . . . Auntie Bintu, these were young boys. Where would they find the money and, even if they did find the money, how could they be sure that there would be constant electricity? This is not England you know.'

'Hmmm. I know, my sister. We have so many headaches. In the old days, there were refrigerators that used kerosene. They were messy but they worked and were invaluable in the rural areas.'

'I have never seen fridges like that. I wonder why we don't have more of those now that our electricity is always failing?' Amina paused for a moment. 'Those were before Independence when many of the European quarters were occupied by European expatriates. Now our people want electricity all the way. As a result the power stations are overloaded and we have cuts.'

'Amina, you never cease to amaze me. So that is the main reason. One hears of cuts and cuts without knowing the reason why.'

Amina nodded. 'So you see why Afam and his friends could not afford to buy one and even if they had bought one, there was no guarantee that there would be power to work it.'

'What did he do then? He did not start mugging people did he?'

'No, Auntie Bintu, but he got his clever idea, only Allah knows how he got it, that with a loan from the bank, he would start a really flourishing business that would make him richer than his brother Osita. His friends fuelled his imagination. They told him that with a name like his — a name that is very meaningful, a name that his grandfather and father had made respectable in the community — that with a name like that the bank manager of the local Union Bank would lend him anything he wanted.

'I don't think Afam had any idea as to what his business was going to be. All he could see was that people who did not go to school at all got contracts from government ministries, so what about him — he at least had spent several years in private schools. He did not see any obstacles and he day-dreamt a good deal. He stopped going to the farm. Now he did not make any pretence about it. If people should say, "Afam why aren't you in the fields helping your grandfather's workers?" he would snap, "Because I am created for bigger things."

'He told himself that, for going to places like the bank, he needed a good suit. He did not have one. Now he started regretting not being on good terms with his father, Charles. He could perhaps have borrowed his father's suit.'

'So, Amina, Charles had not put on weight?'

'No, Auntie Bintu. Even when I saw him years afterwards, he was as trim as I remembered him as a child. Charles was of medium height, very slight, but his slightness gave him the look of a tall person. And as if to emphasise his tallness he tended to stoop sometimes. He was fair, and wore glasses which fitted him as if he had been born with them.

'His son Osita by Maria had the same slightness, but he was even fairer than his father, and taller. Oh, Osita was handsome. And, come to think of it, Afam was not bad looking either. He was broad and strong. He was not very tall, just like his father Charles, but when he was around you got the impression of a solid, healthy lad. He had mostly grown up in the open air, in Ibusa, where he had the wild forests for company most of the time and that really helped his physical development. He had the fine, small facial features which Charles and Osita shared. His mouth was wide and his lips very full, to match his rather broad face. Whereas Osita and Charles had high brows, Afam's was low like his mother's and his brows very thick.'

'The way you describe Afam makes me think that he probably was cut out to be a village farmer, with so much strength.'

Amina thought for a while and then agreed. 'Maybe so, but how can a person like a Permanent Secretary allow his son to be a farmer? People would say that he did not love him because he was not Maria's son.'

'What I don't understand is why we Africans look down on farming. People here still think it's very degrading. I think I told you that the English Queen's son-in-law is a farmer, and he is a gentleman.'

'Well, here most farmers are poor, so we look down on farmers,' Amina said.

'So I see, and we end up importing most of our food even though Allah has given us a very fertile region of the earth.'

'Well, Auntie, you can't blame the youth. When they see people who do not work riding around in big cars and showing off their wealth, they too want to acquire luxuries like that, so they run into the cities looking for contracts.'

'Oh, Amina, we are straying into politics again! But I like it when you bring me up to date about Nigerian affairs. So this is not just what is happening in the Ubakanma family. Do you realise that a whole two years have passed since you told me the story of that unfortunate man Ramonu?'

'I read and re-read the book *Naira Power* and I gave all the copies you sent me away because I did not want my husband Nurudeen to see it at first.'

'I am sorry Amina, I hope I did not cause any trouble between you and my brother Nuru just by writing the story you told me.'

'No, Auntie Bintu, you indirectly strengthened our marriage, because from that story, he knew my past, which I had been carrying with me all the time. Now we can talk about it, though it was sad, but we can laugh about it sometimes, and try to use the lesson we learned from the tragic death of Ramonu as a guide to the way we live now. That is why I am telling you Afam's story as well.

'Anyway he wanted a suit to wear to the bank but pride would not let him go to his father Charles because he had said hurtful things to him. So he went to his mother in her new home. He told Obioma that the bank manager had promised him the money and that it would be bad manners for him to go and see him in his everyday clothes or in a loin cloth.

' "But I have no money," Obioma cried. "I only prepare *gari* for sale, and you know, my son that it is a back-breaking job. I have no money."

'Afam pleaded and pleaded and reminded Obioma that this was the only favour he had ever asked her. He progressed from pleading to being rude, then he became really abusive. He asked his mother whether she was too stupid to see the type of family she was marrying into when she married Charles. He reminded her that she did so because she was greedy and in search of a soft life. He said to her that after she had had him and his little sister, she had to take off with another family because the simple sacrifice many mothers make for their children was beyond her. She had had to leave because again she was in search of a soft life. And now while Maria was in

Lagos sleeping on gold-plated beds, she was here frying cassava to make *gari* in this hot weather. With that he marched off, leaving Obioma with so much guilt.'

'Poor woman, poor mother, what could she do?'

'I know, Auntie Bintu, what could she do? But she did do something. She went to her age-group meeting and borrowed money from them.'

'Oh yes, I always forget the financial power those women have. Do they still have such meetings to help each other?'

'Yes, Auntie Bintu, it is still very common in the villages and the groups are very strong. They help each other in businesses from their contributions; they help one another in bereavement and in sickness and also advise each other. So Obioma went to her group and, though some of them were doubtful about the son's chances of getting money from the bank, they all agreed that she should give him at least something to ease her guilt. "And you never know," some of her friends said, "he may make it. And if he makes it, Afam is not the type of boy to forget his mother because he was more or less brought up here in Ibusa and he knows how things are here with women. So help him as much as you can, and may your god help him to do well in the business he has chosen."

'But what business it was and how he was going to go about it, Obioma did not know and was too timid to ask. She gave the money to Afam to buy his new suit.

14 *The bank loan*

'Auntie Bintu, the more I think about things the more I know that most people are not all bad or all good. There are shades of grey in all of us.'

'Yes, Amina, that is why we see people condemned to death for horrible crimes still praying to Allah for forgiveness, and when you hear their loved ones speak about them you wonder if they could have been the same people. It happens, yes it does.'

Amina nodded, agreeing with me. 'It was like that with Afam. After saying all those horrid things to his mother, he probably thought that he would never see her again because he had offended her far too much.

'Poor boy, he did not know the power of a mother's bond to her child. You are allowed to send away a bad servant or sell a wicked slave. But what can you do with your child but to pull it to yourself and love and forgive it? Afam probably did not know of the depth of his mother's concern until that day.

'Afam, who by then had stopped going to the farm altogether, was sitting under the shade of a palm tree with his friends when his mother counted two hundred naira notes into his hand. "Go and buy the suit, but make sure the tailor uses good material and let him make it big for you because you are still growing."

'Before Afam could recover from the shock, Obioma

had disappeared, a worn-out young woman in a piece of worn-out *abada* cloth. Afam soon recovered himself and ran after his mother. "Thank you, Mother. I shall repay you this money, over and over again. I am sorry for all I said, I did not mean it."

'Obioma turned round and looked at this son she had had for Charles Ubakanma. He had grown so fast that she was sure his body had grown faster than his brain. Looking at him she prayed inwardly that his brain should catch up with the rest of him soon. She then smiled. That smile hid all her anxiety; how was she going to pay back all that money without killing herself with work? How she wished Afam had taken his father's advice and stayed at school. But aloud she said mildly, "Go away with you, Afam, and spend the money wisely."

' "I will, Mother, I will, you'll see," Afam replied. And in that evening sun Afam hugged his mother, like any other child would. This was a gesture that surprised both mother and son, because Afam had never been a person to demonstrate his affection openly.

'Obioma laughed a genuine laugh as if to say, well, after all this, I can now go and grate and fry *gari* for another twelve months with joy.

'Afam was thoughtful. It now occurred to him that he was responsible for his mother and his little sister and maybe his father too — he was not getting younger. He swore to himself on his slow walk back to his friends that he would make it; he would be rich. Then for the first time the thought struck him that maybe it had been unwise to leave school, especially the last place his father got him, at St Thomas's. But, despite his thoughtfulness, he was determined he was never going to allow his father to know his regret. This he kept to himself.

'Afam chose a tailor's stall with "London Tailor" written in front of it. This man from Onitsha sold material and then made it into suits. Afam was lucky for he was not cheated. The tailor was obviously impressed by his youth and must have wondered why a boy with such money could not have ordered his suit from London or have it made in Lagos.'

'Ah, you are wrong, Amina. Some of those Ibo tailors in the market are very good indeed. They hurry their jobs, yes, but the end product can sometimes be very good.'

'I know, Auntie Bintu. Most of the wares sold in Aba and Onitsha markets with "Made in England" on them, are not made in England at all, they're made locally. We all know that but since they look as good as those made abroad, who is complaining?'

'Then why can't they just put "Made in Nigeria" on them?'

'Oh Auntie Bintu, hear what you are saying. When everybody wants to buy things with "Made in England" on them, how do you think somebody selling things with "Made in Nigeria" would fare? Nobody will patronise him. That was why Afam chose the tailor with "London Tailor" in front of his stall. I don't know whether he asked any of his friends' advice, but, as I said, the material was good, it was light tropical woollen stuff, light grey in colour.'

'Oh, Amina, were you there? How can you describe the colour and texture so accurately?'

'No, Auntie Bintu, but I attended Osita's wedding, and Afam was serving and helping and was very happy that day. He wore the suit, so I know. Don't you believe me?'

'I do, Amina, but we must hurry. It's getting late. We must not let my brother have a reason to say that I have taken you away from your wifely duties — though you need breaks like this once in a while. Please go on.'

'Auntie Bintu, Afam looked the picture of confidence and health when he put on his suit. He had been to the local barber for a wet-look cut, and had on a white tie. He even bought dark sunglasses, to make him look like those young executives he had seen in the movies. It must have been towards the end that he began to wonder what he was going to sell. He saw people around him moulding cement blocks for sale, many selling drinks like coca cola and beer, others selling cloth, but he could not put his hand on what he would like to sell. So when one of his friends said simply, "Why don't you say that you wish to import and export?" he thought that the words 'import and export' sounded nice. Nice enough to impress the bank manager.'

'But import and export what?'

'I don't think he knew that the bank manager would ask him that question. It was a cool morning when he set off to the bank. He saw the usual knot of people waiting outside for their money. It is a small bank that usually runs out of money for investors. So if you want a fairly large amount, you have to be there very, very early. And there people did not queue the way you said they do in the UK. Here it is muscle power that counts. Afam was strong. He pushed and fought his way to the front and was confronted by a man in a blue uniform who asked him belligerently what he wanted.

' "I want to see the bank manager," Afam replied in a small voice. Nobody warned him that it was going to be this difficult. "I want to see the bank manager," his voice sang again.

' "Yes, young man, what do you want to see the bank manager for?"

' "You're not even the bank manager. I want to discuss things with him," Afam cried tactlessly, remembering all the trouble he had taken to buy his suit and do his hair, only to be stopped by a man who looked like a gateman or something like that. "I am the son of Ubakanma the Permanent Secretary," Afam added to impress.

'If the man was taken aback, he hid it. He decided to make fun of Afam.

' "So you're the son of Ubakanma?" He wanted to add, "but your father does not own the bank," but checked himself just in case his father was a friend of his boss. He took the easy way out and said, "How do I know you are his son? Anybody can walk in here and say that he is the son of the military governor, but how do I know that the person is not a robber or a killer? Do you have any proof?"

'Afam was now embarrassed. If he had to go through all this for the gateman, what was going to happen when he reached the big man himself? But luck was with him. You know that Ibusa is a close-knit town where people all know each other. A woman from the crowd shouted to the gateman, "Let the child pass. He is Ubakanma's second son. Let him pass."

'Afam went through into a darkened room and had to spend almost half an hour straightening his rumpled suit and deflated pride. He sat next to several well-to-do men who looked rather anxious and agitated. He did not know what air to put on, confidence or fear. What was he going to tell the big man? He bit his nails until they almost bled. After about an hour, the first man was called. Another hour passed, and Afam's feeling of anxiety turned to a feeling of anger. He was still there five hours later, so he gripped the arm of the girl that called out names and asked, "Look, what about me? I have been here since nine o'clock and it's now two. When do I see the big man?"

' "Which big man?" the short-skirted girl asked innocently.

' "How many big men do you have in there?" Afam asked, getting angry. He was tired, he was hungry and he was becoming disappointed.

' "I don't know, you tell me," was the reply he got. He would have let the girl go, but for the derisive laughter that came from the onlookers. Something snapped inside him, and he pulled the girl roughly. She screamed of course, and that brought in more men.

'They handled Afam roughly; some pushed him, others called him bank robber, and tried to force him out of the building. He made use of his physical strength. He was not going to leave the building until he had seen the bank manager. When the confusion and arguments got rather heated, a cool looking man with a neat haircut who was wearing a cool khaki jungle-suit came out from the room inside. As soon as this man made his appearance, there was instant quiet.

' "Now what is the matter? Can't one work in peace in this place?"

' "It's this young man, sah, em say em wan see

you," the man in a blue uniform said, bowing his head at the same time.

'The cool man ignored him and fixed his piercing brown eyes on Afam. He had no smile on his face, and he felt no enthusiasm. He wore a face that was bored.

' "Yes?" he asked Afam, arching one of his brows. "Who do you wish to see and why are you making all this noise and causing so much disturbance? Don't you know that we look after other people's money here? Don't you know that bank robbers like disturbances like this? Who do you want anyway?"

' "You, the bank manager. I would like to see the bank manager, sah!" Afam said quickly before the man left.

'The man turned his back and Afam made as if to follow him inside his private office thinking that his silence meant that he should do so. Then the man turned his head and asked in a bored voice, "And where are you going, young man?"

' "I want to see the bank manager."

'Then a wicked smile spread over the man's fleshy, over-fed face. "The bank manager! The bank manager! The bank manager! He is not on seat."

'As Afam was bundled out of the building, he could hear the mocking laughter of the girl secretary, the man in uniform and the onlookers. This time he could put up no resistance. They threw him out and he quickly picked himself up and began to dust his now dirty and mud-splashed suit. It was then that the man in uniform brought him the small leather case, which Afam had bought at Asaba market to complete his young executive image.

'He snatched the case from the man, who laughed at him once more. Then someone from the crowd asked him in a confidential tone, "What did you want to see the bank manager for?"

' "I wanted to see if he could give me some money to start a business."

' "Who told you to come to the bank? Have you no people? Well, if you want to get the money from the bank, you must do it the proper way, not by forcing your way in. The manager won't see you that way."

' "Which is the proper way?" Afam asked, his voice rising in excitement.

'People laughed at his naivety. They said, "Look at him asking the proper way to see a good man. You give his gateman a good handshake, and give the big man another thirst-cooler, and then he will see you."

'Afam understood what they meant. So, undaunted, he returned the following day, in his now not-so-smart suit. As soon as he saw the gateman he shook his hand with two naira notes, and let him see the bottle of whisky he had for his master.'

'Where did he get the whisky from Amina?'

'I don't know, Auntie Bintu. You know that a person like the Obi would keep a cellar full of all kinds of drinks for his visitors. Afam probably just helped himself.'

'He must have, because whisky is very, very expensive here.'

'I know, Auntie Bintu, it can cost over fifteen naira. Anyway, because of the handshake to the gateman and the thirst-quencher to the big man, the gateman and the secretary did not delay him, and the bank manager was on seat.

'The big man encouraged Afam to talk himself dry. He was able to judge that Afam was not popular with his father, because he knew Charles personally, and he had never mentioned that he had another son. He could tell from Afam's rough behaviour that he was the skeleton in Ubakanma's family cupboard. At length, he promised to write to him and let him know. Afam, who was too eager, wanted to know right there whether the sum of five thousand naira would be allowed him soon. The big man simply smiled, thanked him for his whisky, and promised to write to him.

'So Afam waited days and days, but no reply came. Poor boy, I think he's still waiting.'

'Hmmmm, that's the way of the world. And if he showed up there, they would accuse him of wanting to rob a bank. Do you blame such people when they become bitter? The man was wrong. He should at least have written to him to say that he would not be given the loan.'

'Well, Auntie Bintu, word has it that he probably wrote, but signs are that he did not. Anyway that was what Afam said much later.

'The truth was that he never got the loan; it would have been irresponsible to give it to him. But Afam was not to know that and in his mind he felt he had been cheated. Growing up can be so painful if one wants to do it all alone. He should have told his father. But he bottled up his bitterness.

15 The wedding

'The day Ruth, Osita's fiancée, returned from England, Auntie Bintu, one would have thought that Maria had just had a new baby. She invited most of her friends to Murtala Muhammed Airport. Though the plane was slightly delayed her friends were willing to wait all night if necessary. Everyone was so happy for her and very proud of knowing her and her charming doctor son, Osita.

'The plane soon landed and with curiosity and joy people craned their necks to see what Ruth looked like. She did not let Maria down. She wore a pale coloured cotton suit, you know, those summer ones that are not tight yet show off a slim girl's figure. Her hair looked natural but you could tell that it was a look achieved with patience and care. As soon as she saw the crowd waiting for her, she opened up herself to receive all her well wishers. She smiled, she kissed, she embraced, and people felt comfortable with her. There was none of the stuffiness about her which one notices in some of those who have stayed a long time in the UK.'

'Eh, watch it! I hope you are not referring to me and my family, young lady?'

Amina laughed, sucking at the gaps in her teeth. 'Oh, Auntie Bintu, you know what I mean. I am not referring to you, otherwise I would not have said it to your face. But you must agree that some of your people do put on airs, don't they?'

'That was a long time ago, not these days when everybody goes to London at the weekends or during sales.'

'Well, I won't argue with you, Auntie Bintu. But I live in Nigeria and I know that only a few people can go to summer sales in London. You often see those who can afford to go to your Oxford Street, and you get the impression that we all do it. I have never been to London for instance, and our living standards are a little above the average for Nigerians. Those you talk about are the cream of our society. As I was saying about Ruth, she was received almost like royalty. There were parties in her parents' house at Surulere, and parties at Maria's in Ikoyi and parties at Osita's at Satellite city. It was a month of parties for Ruth, and during that time, the young couple found that they could not bear to be separated. It was at first planned that Ruth should do her Youth Service before getting married, but everybody was impatient. Maria could not wait to see her first grandchild; Ruth's parents were frightened she might get pregnant and ruin the beautiful clean girl image she had so far created. And as for Osita, he worried everybody to do something to hasten the wedding day.

'The only obstacle was that Ruth, who was a Doctor of Psychology, wanted to be a working girl. She was nice, but a very modern girl.'

'Well I do not blame her. Do you know how long it took her to qualify? Why should she throw it all away simply because she was marrying Osita?'

'Exactly. So Osita saw to it that she could do her Youth Service in Lagos, just as if she was working.

Soon, they fixed the wedding day. Again the couple had to be blessed in different places. They were Catholics, so they first married here at Holy Cross, then went to Ibusa to be blessed in the native way by Obi Ubakanma who, because of an illness, could not come to Lagos. It was lovely. But what moved me most of all were Ruth's bridesmaids. They were her college friends from the University and they travelled all the way from England to be with their friend. I thought that was beautiful and yet strange.'

'How do you mean, "strange", Amina?'

'You know they being white and Ruth black. It made the official picture stick in my memory somehow.'

'It is not strange at all. As long ago as the early seventies, when I was a student, I was a bridesmaid to a very close friend of mine. We shared a room when we were undergraduates. She and her husband are white, and I was the only maid, but her two little sisters were her flower girls.'

'Really? As far back as that, and in England? I thought that was the time they were sticking "Blacks go home" on all their buses?'

'Most white people would say "Blacks go home" even now in the eighties. I don't know about sticking it on their buses, but I know that many landladies were not particularly keen on black tenants. And, Amina, if anyone tells you that things have changed, tell that person that she is living in a dreamland. They have not changed, but many things are changing very quickly around them so they are forced to pretend to be changing at least superficially.'

'In that case, Auntie Bintu, things have not progressed then. You come again to my point. They are racist over there, hence we were surprised their daughters could come to a black colleague's wedding all the way from the UK.'

'Well we are now independent, are we not? And we are an oil nation, even though we may be experiencing some minor hiccups, but they will smooth over. Nonetheless we are now a nation to reckon with, so that has gone a long way in helping to alter the image of the black person.'

'Amina, if we go all political again, we'll forget Afam and his family.'

'That is why we in Africa are born storytellers. We deviate on purpose to lengthen and enrich the suspense and then come back to the story line. You know why, because we think the whole world is linked to one another. You cannot tell a whole story in isolation; for to us no one should live in isolation.'

'I write books, Amina, and in England they like their writers to concentrate on the main character and not deviate too much.'

'Well, their life is like that, is it not? When you marry, you care only for your husband, and his people do not matter. When you move into a new neighbourhood, you mind your own business. You may not know the name of your next-door neighbour even if you have lived there for years. That is how they are. We are not like that and that is why I think our ways are better. Each one is responsible for the other.'

'Yes, Amina, so did Afam go to his brother's wedding?'

'Oh, Auntie Bintu, did I not tell you? Well, when the wedding day was fixed, Osita went up to his parents and said that the wedding would not take place if

Charles and Maria did not allow Afam to be his best man.'

'Did they tell Osita that Afam was simply wandering about doing nothing?'

'I don't think so. But Afam was not bad looking and Charles was in a dilemma. He did not want that boy Afam to come to Lagos and stay with them again. And he could not trust him to stay with Osita, because somehow Charles knew that there was bound to be that brotherly jealousy he was trying to avoid.'

'Well, Charles caused it. If he had remained firm and accepted Maria's disability as his own and counted Allah's blessing there would not have been Afam.'

'Oh well, Auntie Bintu, he had to live up to his name. Uba-ka-nma, a large family is better. As I said, Charles and Maria did not know how to voice out their fears, but then they thought that Afam, seeing his successful brother Osita, might be encouraged to do better. "And you never know, Maria, he has probably grown out of his verbal violence," Charles said, with the dreamy optimism of most parents over their offspring.

'What they did not know, Auntie Bintu, was that after the bad treatment Afam had got from the bank manager in Ibusa, he had become very cynical and was hardening rapidly for a boy of his age.

'He did not wait to be invited twice. He cleaned his new suit and got to Lagos within seventy hours of his receiving the invitation. He was glad to see his brother and Ruth and he looked good on the day of the wedding. The two men looked really handsome on that day. Afam was becoming bigger, and Osita had already got a thin academic look and his glasses seemed to put the final stamp on his western breeding. But Afam's grin was wide, he was full of life, he was loud, and he was strong. He was all right, so much so that Charles started congratulating himself on agreeing with Osita. And Afam behaved well.

'The young couple went off on honeymoon to Disneyland in California; it was the time of the great Olympics held in America. And Osita, though not a sportsman, liked watching athletics of all kinds. He himself had swum for a while while he was in England, but he never made it to the Olympics. So he liked watching.'

'Fancy going to the Olympics for a honeymoon.'

'Auntie Bintu, he did not take part. Well, I know what you mean. But they were not strangers to each other. They had probably lived together in England. There people do not ask too many questions, do they? And guess what, they left their new, well-furnished flat to Afam to look after until their return!'

16 *Afam's dreams*

'It was while Osita and Ruth were in California that Afam suddenly realised that, by shutting himself away in Ibusa, he was missing a great deal out of life. He looked up his old friends and to his horror he realised that those of them who were not in educational institutions building their futures, were working and had become respectable. Those wild pranks they had played as young boys were simply because they were young boys. It made Afam look as if he was suffering from a case of arrested development. Most of them were nice and polite to him but as soon as they knew that he had done nothing to help himself, they started to shy away from his company.

'Fed up with being alone admiring his brother's maisonette flat, and fingering his shiny Peugeot car, Afam decided that he was going to start the business which had been denied him in Ibusa here in Lagos. He would no longer deal with foreign goods but would open a drinks bar in Ibusa. But again he needed money. To approach Charles and Maria was out of the question for he guessed he knew that they would say, "Did we not tell you so?" And the mere thought of another confrontation with his father sent poisoned and bitter juices down his young veins. He had acquired new friends and he was advised to ask his brother Osita when he returned from his honeymoon.

'The day Osita and Ruth returned from Los Angeles, the sun was shining. It was shining all over Lagos and one look at the happy couple showed that it was shining on their faces and in their hearts as well. And for the first time, Afam showed signs of jealousy when he was relegated to the guest room. He had been using the master bedroom when his brother and his new wife were away.'

'Did they tell him off for doing that, Amina?'

'No, Auntie Bintu, they did not. As I have so far hinted, though Osita was trained abroad, he was not stuffy. He did not mind his brother sleeping in their room and Afam had not taken anything away. But as soon as they returned then it dawned on Afam that the type of rich happiness that Osita was enjoying might never be his. He suppressed his fear and jealousy, but kept deluding himself that if only someone would lend him money to start his business, he would catch up with Osita.'

'Poor boy, he did not know that there is so much more to education than paper certificates. He could never be Osita, he should have tried to find himself and love himself as he was and not ape another person.'

'Well, Auntie Bintu, he was too young to know that and Charles was too busy living his own life now he was enjoying the reflected glory of being the father of a good and successful son. He had done all he could with Afam, and his failure was of his own making. As far as he was concerned, when Osita and Ruth returned, Afam should have gone back to Ibusa to be a farmer. But Afam did not want that kind of life, not after he had seen the way Osita lived and having heard what his new friends told him, that doctors do get a lot of money, especially those in Lagos. He had kicked himself and wondered where he had got the idea of poor doctors from.'

'Most people go into the profession because of the prestige it gives, not the money any more. In the olden days, this was so, but now, doctors are almost like everybody else. They still have the glamour but not the old power especially now that there are so many branches of medicine. But in Osita's case, his mother probably helped him in setting up his maisonette flat.'

'Auntie Bintu, you know exactly what happened. Maria ordered all the furniture for her son as wedding presents. She even paid for his first car, so Osita had more money to spend on himself, unlike his colleagues whose advance on cars had to be deducted from their pay. Osita did not have to accept the government furniture as well. There was a stamp of individuality in his surroundings. Oh, Auntie Bintu, what would a loving mother not do for a good child?

'Afam waited a few days, toying with the best way to approach his brother. But only four days after their return, Charles called all of them to dinner. Afam looked open-mouthed at his father's living standards and felt like saying, "You all live this way and left me to rot in Ibusa."

'Charles' voice soon cut through into his inattention. "Afam, you'll have to go back soon. You know what Ibusa labourers are. When the cat is away the mice will play."

'Afam looked at all of them sitting at the table with sad eyes like those of a thirsty cat. His mouth at first seemed glued together with bitterness. Then, when he opened his mouth, he began to accuse everybody except himself. "You want me out of the way, Father,

because I have no job, because I am an embarrassment to you all. You invited me to Osita's wedding
to show off to me all that you have, and now you want
me to go back to work on the farm and look after your
dying father. I know what you planned for me . . . ''

'Osita could not believe his ears. He had been
brought up to respect his father. He knew Charles had
made wrong decisions in the past, but he was human
like everybody else. And there was one thing he could
not stand and that was raised voices at the dinner
table. He got up and said in a low quivering voice,
"Shut up, Afam, just shut up. You had every
opportunity to be anything you wanted but you lost
it. Would you apologise to the ladies and to Father
immediately.''

'Afam, who had been used to telling people what
he felt, believed that, as long as one could get away
with it, one could say anything to anyone. He
respected his father, yes but his father was Maria's
husband. He had seen them go into their bedroom
when he was little. He had quietly listened to their
love-making and felt his heart torn when he grew up
and knew that he wanted his own mother to be where
Maria was — by his father's side. And he knew that
it was Maria who would not let his mother live with
them, because Charles was afraid of losing her. And
now here was Maria's son telling him to apologise.
Apologise for what? Was he not speaking the truth.
So he simply ignored Osita and went on eating his
dessert as if Osita's voice was just like water washing
down the back of a duck.

' "I say you should apologise Afam," Osita repeated,
his thin body shaking with anger, so much so that
Ruth placed her hand on his shoulder to calm him.

' "Don't worry. Mamma and I are not offended. Don't worry. Just calm down. Two wrongs never make a right. But, Afam, you must leave in the morning for the Ibusa farm. You can make it as a farmer. You have help, you have good land and you have health and youth. Excuse me everybody." And with that Charles left the table, with Maria following him. Ruth pulled Osita away as well. And you know something, I don't think that was right. They should have stayed there and argued it out with him. But they did not. They behaved like Europeans, because of Osita and Ruth, I think.

'Afam stared at the dinner table for a while, then suddenly he was overcome with anger and frustration. With one big sweep, he smashed all Maria's best china which she had used to prepare the welcome dinner for her son and his new wife Ruth.'

'Oh, my God, why did Afam have to do that?'

'Well, who knows what goes on in the mind of a frustrated young person? Maria and Ruth were so shocked that the two women simply clung to each other. And as for Ruth, a chill ran through her. She said later that on that night, she felt that what Afam had done was a bad omen. But she was too scared to say a word, being a new wife and still regarded as very young.

'The servants came in to clear up the broken china which Maria had been collecting long before Osita was born. She could never replace it, but what could a woman do? Her husband wanted another son, now he'd got Afam; what could she do?

'Then, mechanically, Ruth bent down, picked up one piece of the gravy boat, and tried to stick it to the other bits. She realised the futility of her wishes and began to cry as she allowed the bits to fall and break into smaller pieces.

'Ruth, who normally had a firm control over her emotions, was really surprisesd at herself. Osita was embarrassed and in the heat of the moment he had to say something. He announced that Ruth and himself had been wanting to say something all evening. He gently led Ruth to a chair and said, "Mother, Father, I am sorry to be so dramatic, but we are going to have babies ... em Ruth and myself." He felt sheepish and he knew he looked it, for he put his two palms on his cheeks, waiting to see everybody's reaction.

'Maria jumped up from her chair, almost colliding with the coffee table placed in the centre of the room. "What do you mean, sorry? And what do you mean by babies?" she cried happily.

'The whole situation suddenly became magically funny especially as Ruth was now laughing with the tears of sadness at the loss of the china plates still on her face. And instead of Osita answering his mother's questions, he said to Ruth, "You know something, you really look silly, laughing and crying at the same time."

'But she did not look silly any more when Charles, Maria and even Osita started to do the same thing. They got carried away, so much so that Afam, who was standing by the door that led out to the dining room, had never in all his life felt more like a stranger in his family.

'They became aware of his presence when the door was quietly shut. And that quiet closing of the door brought a chill to their hearts as they stared at each other. There was no doubt now that Afam had become

the great skeleton in Ubakanma's family cupboard.
And no one could tell when he would pop out again
with a semblance of life.

17 *Woman as an individual*

'It was a pitch dark night. It was moonless but very hot. There would have been silence but for the myriad night noises made by fireflies and mosquitoes. Ruth moved from Osita who was deep in sleep. She wanted to tell him so many little things she had been feeling about their expected twins. She could feel the lumps and knots they were making in her stomach and was tempted to take Osita's hand and place it on her belly. But she knew that would be selfish. He had apparently had a very busy day at the Lagos General Hospital and would be up early in the morning. Instead she began rubbing her hands on her belly herself and began to smile at the stars which she could see through all their glass windows.

'Then suddenly there was a thud, like the fall of a bag full of *gari* . She stopped her movement and wondered what the noise might be. Then there was silence, yet she found it difficult to go back to sleep. "Gosh it is hot," she gasped. If only Osita would allow her to have the air-conditioner on all night, life would not have been so bad. But he had this belief that air-conditioning was bad for her in her condition. So they had to sleep in this heat and under an old-fashioned mosquito net, not dissimilar to those favoured by the old European missionaries.

'Then, like a bolt, she shot up. Somebody was

watching her! She could not see the person and for a moment she felt disinclined to put on the light. But she knew there was somebody there. Another thud followed, and a strong grip snatched the hand she stretched out to put on the bed switch. She screamed. Osita woke and to this day, she could not recall the sequence of the next few fatal minutes in detail. But she kept telling them in court . . . '

'In court, Amina, why in court?'

'Oh, Auntie Bintu, be patient. I shall soon finish the story. Ruth was sure she heard Afam's voice raised and panicky speaking to the other men, saying something like, "Take everything, he wears a watch, take it all, but don't harm him, no don't kill my brother, no, no, don't kill my brother: I only need some money for the business." She was sure the man who was holding her and making her sniff a piece of cotton wool saturated with choloroform was Afam.'

'Oh my God, Amina, they did not kill Osita, did they?'

Amina sighed, and we both started to wipe the tears that were in our eyes. I did not have the courage to ask her what happened next. I could guess.

We looked around and saw that we were the only ones left. All the other customers had gone. And to our horror, the serving boy who had wanted to know whether we were 'business' women was approaching us with a sickening smile. Behind him was the barrel-bellied man, waddling from side to side like an overfed duck.

'Amina, let's go. I can't face that young man again.'

The car was still there, and stepping into the bright sunshine from the cool interior of the restaurant was like coming into a completely different world. Amina had for the past couple of hours completely mesmerised me with this sad, sad story.

'Can you manage the car?' I asked rather anxiously.

'Yes, Auntie Bintu. All this happened three months ago. I am only telling you now because I went to see Ruth and her two bouncing babies last week. They are both boys, and they now belong to Maria and Ruth. It looks as if Allah was replacing all the lost men in Ubakanma's compound.'

'What do you mean, all the lost men, Amina?'

'Apparently when Afam saw that his friends had killed his brother, he got mad and started to attack them just like an enraged animal. The friends were frightened, because they knew that, if they were caught, they would hang. And the only way to be sure of not being found out was to silence Afam. One hammer blow finished him just outside the door leading to Osita's lovely flat.

'And as if that was not enough, Charles heard what had befallen Osita the following day, and he took many sleeping tablets, by accident they said, and of course he never woke again. The Obi lived for four weeks after this and followed his son and grandsons.'

'Hmm Amina, but why can't we be satisfied with what Allah has given us?'

'That is exactly what everybody has been asking ever since. Because his name was Ubakanma — a large family is better — I think he wanted to live up to his name, he ended up having no children at all.'

'Not quite so, Auntie Bintu, Maria and Ruth seemed quite determined to raise those two babies, for is that not what most women are condemned into doing? Raising men only to have them destroyed in front of their mothers and wives either through unnecessary wars or through greed? And it's always left to us women to start all over again to keep the race going.'

'Ah, but the Obi did not see the twins, so he died thinking that he had lost everything. But that girl Ruth, will she stay with her mother-in-law? After all she is young, beautiful and intelligent. Men will start harassing her soon.'

'Maybe so, Auntie Bintu, but she is one of these new determined women who never undervalue themselves. I'm sure she'll have men friends, but she's going to stay loyal to her Osita. She was only saying the other day, "Thank God I have my career." '

'And that I think is the saviour of modern woman . . . a career, however modest.'

'There I agree with you, Auntie Bintu. Raising a few kids is not enough for a modern woman. She should have a career as well, however humble.'

With this Amina turned into the slow-moving traffic at Mile Two as we made our way to Festac city in Lagos.

Amina smiled and said, 'Thanks for a lovely meal, Auntie Bintu.'

'And thank you for another lovely story, Amina. I am going to call this a kind of marriage because in my mind, I think Ruth, Maria and the twins have a kind of marriage and family. The two women have now got into a kind of marriage. May Allah help them with the twins, and may they be like their father Osita, but may they live long to see their great grandchildren.'

'Amen, Amen, Amen,' Amina sang with one hand uplifted to Allah.

Then suddenly she asked, 'Auntie, what do we need men for really?'

'We need them to give us babies, and after that I don't know . . . '

'And Auntie, do they not say that you can now have babies, without men, you know . . . '

'Shush, Amina. That is not a nice thing to say.'